'Am I being offered the use of a spare bedroom?'

Paige had tilted her head and now she gazed up at him speculatively. 'Or should I be preparing myself for possible seduction attempts?'

'I don't know.' Josh laughed. 'I haven't decided yet. Just out of interest, how does one prepare oneself for possible seduction attempts?'

'One shaves one's legs,' she said smartly. 'Only I've forgotten my razor.'

'I'll buy you a new one,' he said calmly, getting confirmation, if he'd needed it, that her flirtatious banter had merely been meant jokingly from the quick, half-startled, very green look his comment had provoked. 'Just in case.' He shut the car door firmly on her suddenly alarmed expression. 'You never can tell.'

A New Zealand doctor with restless feet, **Helen Shelton** has lived and worked in Britain and travelled widely. Married to an Australian she met while on safari in Africa, she recently moved to Sydney, where they plan to settle for a little while at least. She has always been an enthusiastic reader and writer, and inspiration for the background for her Medical Romances™ comes directly from her own experiences working in hospitals in several countries around the world.

Recent titles by the same author:

HEART AT RISK
COURTING CATHIE*
IDYLLIC INTERLUDE
A TIMELY AFFAIR

*Bachelor Doctors

THE BEST MAN

BY
HELEN SHELTON

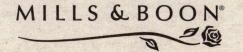

MILLS & BOON®

All the characters in this book have no existence outside the imagination of the author, and have no relation whatsoever to anyone bearing the same name or names. They are not even distantly inspired by any individual known or unknown to the author, and all the incidents are pure invention.

First published in Great Britain 2000
Harlequin Mills & Boon Limited,
Eton House, 18-24 Paradise Road, Richmond, Surrey TW9 1SR

© Poppytech Services Pty Ltd 2000

ISBN 0 263 82272 9

Set in Times Roman 10½ on 11½ pt.
03-0011-53242

Printed and bound in Spain
by Litografia Rosés, S.A., Barcelona

CHAPTER ONE

'MARRIAGE is the greatest invention ever discovered.' David directed a bleary beam at his best man, before taking a slurp from one of the two brimming champagne flutes he clutched. 'I recommend it highly. I am quite possibly one of the happiest men alive.'

'Perhaps also one of the drunkest.' Josh removed the flutes from his friend's clumsy grasp and swapped them for a coffee from a passing waiter. 'Part of a best man's role,' he observed, his mouth quirking at David's forlorn look as he watched his champagne being borne away, 'is making sure you're up to your wedding-night responsibilities.'

'Up to them?' David turned pale and abruptly serious, and Josh realised his friend wasn't as intoxicated as he'd feared. 'Josh, I've been *up* to them for six months,' David said desperately. 'Why else did you think I'd been walking around with this funny look on my face?'

'You mean you and Louise haven't…?' But David's mournful expression meant Josh didn't need to finish. His gaze drifted downwards from the mezzanine level of the hotel to the restaurant where his friend's confident-looking new bride sat laughing with her girlfriends. 'You're kidding.'

'I wish I was,' David said thickly. 'I'm drinking myself stupid, Josh, because I'm nervous as hell.'

'And Louise has never—'

'Never.'

'Not even a—'

'Nothing.' Another waiter offered them champagne and David dumped his coffee and took a flute instead. 'Kisses

5

until I can't see straight, but that's it.' He took a long swallow of the alcohol. 'She's always wanted her wedding night to be perfect.'

'An excellent reason to stay sober.' Josh firmly extracted the champagne from his friend's grasp and returned it to the waiter. 'Relax,' he soothed, retrieving the coffee and passing it back to David. 'It'll be fine.'

'Easy for you to say.' David's mouth twisted. 'Being practical, tonight we can't, not with the flight, but what about tomorrow? What if I can't please Louise?'

Josh smiled. 'Dave, you love Louise, don't you? You're not marrying her just because it's the only way you'll get your hands on her?'

'Of course not.' David looked shocked. 'I love Louise. She's sweet and kind, she's a great nurse and she cooks like an angel. I adore her.'

'And she loves you.'

David blinked down at his bride. 'For some strange reason.'

'For no strange reason.' After all these years he should be used to it, but Josh still found his friend's ever-present self-doubt hard to fathom. 'You're a great person, a terrific doctor, and you'll make an equally terrific husband,' he told him sincerely. 'You love each other so you'll work things out. Drink up, Dave. The coffee, I mean,' he added tersely when the groom sent a longing look in the direction of another champagne-bearing waiter. 'It might help clear your head.'

David's head swivelled back to him. 'Doesn't my best friend have any tips for me?'

'Drink milk for the calcium, choose olive oil for your arteries and take up exercise.' He laughed at David's expression. 'Hey, I'm a surgeon, not a sex counsellor. Just relax. You can't kid me you're not experienced enough to be able to handle things. Do what comes naturally.'

'Doing what comes naturally is going to take about four seconds,' David said dully.

Josh laughed again. 'What's the rush? That's a wedding band you're wearing now and that means you've got the rest of your life with her.'

'I suppose.' But despite his resigned tone David brightened fractionally. 'I suppose there's no urgency.'

'None at all. Although I'd still ease back on the alcohol.'

'Ease back on the booze,' David agreed absently.

'When's your flight?'

'Soon. We leave here at nine.' David was leaning over the balcony now, blowing kisses down at his bride, his beam back in place. 'Being married is terrific,' he blurted. 'Josh, I know you're not going to listen but you should try it some day.'

'I'm thinking about it.'

David's head came up fast. 'What?'

'I'm thinking about it,' Josh repeated evenly.

'What, now?' David looked astonished. 'Now *you're* kidding.'

'Why?' Josh was puzzled by his doubt. To him, it was a decision that made perfect sense. 'I'm thirty-five, too,' he reminded him. 'My career's established and I want children before I'm too old to enjoy them properly. It's time I thought about settling down.'

'But…Josh?' David's mouth had dropped open but then he closed it again. 'You don't mean *Veronica*?'

The name came out almost as a squeal and, glancing down towards where his partner for the afternoon lingered, flirting with one of David's groomsmen, Josh inclined his head. 'Not Veronica,' he conceded, lifting an acknowledging hand when she darted a provocative gaze up towards him. 'We've stopped dating.'

Veronica was a beautiful, intelligent and witty doctor, but although he enjoyed her company and had invited her to partner him to the wedding, their brief romantic relationship had come to an amicable end several weeks before.

'So…do you have someone in mind?'

'No one in particular,' Josh said calmly. 'But I have an idea of what I'm looking for.'

'I can see her already.' David was grinning now. 'Tall, blonde, stunning, intellectual, highly organised, independent and career-minded?'

'You've just described Veronica,' Josh observed mildly. 'I've already told you we're not dating any more.'

'Josh, I've just described *every* woman you've ever dated.'

Not every woman he'd been interested in, Josh registered, but he wasn't about to point out who'd differed from that description. 'Looks aren't important,' he said neutrally. 'I want a mother for my children. All that matters is that she's maternal and loving.'

'But if she can combine everything else, then so much the better, hmm?' His friend was rubbing his hands together. 'Josh, I've got to admit you've surprised me. I thought you enjoyed playing the field too much to ever sacrifice that.'

Josh lifted his eyes briefly to the ceiling. 'Dave, if I played around even a tenth as much as you seem to enjoy thinking I do…'

'I know. I know.' David flapped a dismissive hand in the air. 'You'd still be in med school. I know, Josh. I've heard you before. But nothing you say changes facts. And if I had your experience I wouldn't be nervous about tonight. I've only had four girlfriends.'

'One of whom lasted two years,' Josh pointed out. 'You're hardly inexperienced, Dave. You and Paige lived together for two years at least.'

'We shared a house, Josh. Paige paid rent—irregularly, I admit, at times, because she couldn't always afford to do it dead on time—but she paid in full and she had her own bedroom. She and I weren't involved that long. I liked her a lot but after a few weeks of living together she decided the boyfriend and girlfriend stuff wasn't going to work and she moved into the other bedroom and that was the end of that. I was cut up about it for a long time but she was determined.'

Josh turned cold. 'I didn't know you and Paige weren't sleeping together.'

'Well…I might have misled you a little on that. When we broke up after those first weeks I kept meaning to say something but, you know—' David looked sheepish '—pride and all that. Then once she'd left London there didn't seem any need to explain any more.'

But the last time Josh had seen Paige, six months before she'd left London, they'd met alone, and she'd not said anything to indicate that she and David hadn't been romantically involved. Naturally he'd always assumed—from their closeness, from things David had said and from his obvious adoration of Paige—that the pair had been deeply in love. 'I was sure you were involved all that time.'

'I know.' His friend gave a sort of bleary shrug. 'Sorry. Even after the romance ended I still felt…I suppose *possessive* is the best word. I knew that Paige would have driven me mad if we'd stayed together but I still had feelings for her. She was always so…so *Paige*. So crazy. Nothing like Louise. It wouldn't have worked in the long term but…I don't think I would have coped if she'd gone off with someone else. Particularly not—'

Josh knew what the other man wanted to say and he tensed himself in preparation, but instead David broke off and leaned over the balcony to wave at Louise. 'Paige had a thing for you,' David declared flatly. 'I suspect she knew how pathetic I'd be about it so she tried to hide it. But I knew her pretty well. Didn't you ever suspect?'

'She never said anything.' One of the waiters was still circulating with champagne, and although David didn't take a flute when he came close again Josh did. Apart from the toasts it was his first alcoholic drink of the evening and he gulped half of it. 'Not a thing,' he said, and it was true. But the other truth was that she hadn't needed to say anything. He'd known how she'd felt just as he'd known how much he'd wanted her. But neither of them had done anything about it and there was nothing for David to know.

'I haven't seen in her in almost three years,' he added deliberately. 'Not since about six months before her mother died and she went back to Yorkshire.'

He finished his drink, then looked at his friend steadily. 'Where is Paige now? Is she still in Malton?' He deliberately stopped short of demanding if she was married although, of course, that was what he most wanted to know. 'What's she doing these days?'

'After her mother's funeral she stayed home to look after her father.' David looked pensive for a few seconds. 'We've kept in touch sporadically but I haven't seen her in two years. She should be here. She RSVP'd but, knowing Paige, she probably got the date wrong or she's forgotten or she's found a book she can't bear to stop reading or her car's broken down on the M1 and she's stranded miles away.' He laughed. 'Remember that day she got us stuck out in that heap-of-junk dinghy she'd hired in that lake in the middle of the thunderstorm?'

As vividly as he remembered the way she'd laughed at them for being so afraid. 'Vaguely,' Josh said vaguely, taking another champagne.

'And that awful stray mongrel she tried to foist on me?' his friend teased. 'The flea-bitten one with the lame leg?'

'Tiger's doing just fine,' Josh reminded him dryly, knowing David knew perfectly well that the dog now lived with

Josh's parents in Kent. 'His hip replacement might have cost me a fortune but he's been fine ever since.'

'You liked her, didn't you?'

'Of course I liked her,' Josh said smoothly.

David folded his arms. 'You know what I mean.'

'I hardly knew her.'

'You knew her well enough.' The look David sent him was uncharacteristically shrewd. 'You don't have to tell me because I can tell by your face. Josh, I didn't realise. I thought it was just Paige. I thought it was all on her side. You never said anything. I didn't think…or more likely I didn't want to think. Look, I can give you her number,' he said jerkily. 'If I'd known you were… I'm sorry, I'm bloody thick sometimes. I should have come clean about Paige years ago. It was just stupid selfishness and pride that stopped me at the time. I know she'd love to see you. I mean, she's halfway to being nuts at times and we both know she's not your type for anything long term, but she's still an awful lot of fun…'

'I'll think about it,' Josh prevaricated. He didn't need Paige's number. He'd known it by heart for years. Soon after she'd left London he'd rung directory enquiries for it but, unsure whether Paige's feelings had extended beyond the purely sexual, as well as aware of how badly him becoming involved with her might affect David who'd been mournful for months after her departure, he'd never used it. 'She's not married, then?'

'Not married.' David lifted one shoulder. 'But you know Paige and she knows me. She wouldn't necessarily tell me about a boyfriend.'

On the floor beneath them, the noise level had risen and Josh looked down to catch David's bride waving at them from the crowd gathering for the farewells. He put his glass aside. 'Time for you to be leaving,' he told his friend heavily, when David looked about to say something more. 'All set?'

'Yeah.' David nodded at him, to Josh's relief apparently content to let the issue of Paige ride as they went towards the broad stairs connecting the mezzanine level with the lower one. 'Thanks, Josh. You know. For everything.'

But at Josh's briefly dismissive nod David stopped. 'I mean it,' he persisted, one hand coming out to Josh's arm. 'It's not just the drink talking. I couldn't have had a better friend over the years. You've been there for me through thick and thin regardless of how much of a pest I was making of myself. I want you to know how much I appreciate that.'

'It's been fun, Dave.' Josh slung his arm around his friend's shoulders and delivered him to his new wife. 'All the best. Relax and enjoy yourself.'

'See you in a few weeks.' David lifted his hand to acknowledge the cheers of the reception party as he and Louise moved, their arms entwined, towards the foyer of the hotel.

There was rice-throwing in lieu of the confetti the hotel forbade, and in a blaze of farewells and best wishes the couple were driven away in a long white limousine.

'You look pensive, Josh.' Veronica's hand came around the elbow of his jacket as he lingered, watching them drive out of sight. 'Feeling nostalgic?'

'Nostalgic?'

'End of an era, and all that?'

'Perhaps.' But Josh lifted one shoulder in part-dismissal of further introspection. David's revelations about Paige had left him unsettled—no, more than unsettled, inwardly he was still reeling—but there wasn't anything he could do about that immediately. Or at least there was nothing he *should* do about that immediately. He needed to think. He had to be rational. Three years was a long time. Things had changed for him and Paige herself would have changed. Just because once she'd been able to set his senses dancing simply by looking at him, didn't mean she still could, or that he wanted her to, or even that she would want that power if she still had it.

'Dave and I have been friends since we were toddlers,' he added mildly. 'Our mothers were at school together. It's been a long era.'

'Louise seems sweet.'

'She does.' Josh thought David and his bride were well matched. He didn't know Louise well but she seemed to have the same pleasant way of looking at the world as David, along with the same tendency to believe the best of others. And with Louise, David would always have someone to take care of. That would be important to him. He needed someone who needed him.

Unlike Paige, who'd always have demanded a no-holds-barred equal relationship, he thought heavily, lifting his hand to Veronica's arm as he turned her back towards the sweeping entrance of the hotel. 'Still enjoying yourself or ready for home?'

'Enjoying myself immensely.' She lifted her brows at him mockingly. 'I've met the most charming man. And consider yourself relieved of the obligation to drive me home because he's promised me a ride in his new Bentley.'

'Ah, then that would have to be Martin.' Josh named the groomsman he'd seen her talking with earlier. Martin Stanton was an old friend of David's from medical school. He'd specialised in plastics and was now working as a cosmetic surgeon in what sounded like an extremely lucrative private practice. 'But are you sure a ride home is all he has in mind?'

'I'm quite sure it isn't,' she told him archly, her eyes sparkling. 'And since you've put yourself firmly out of reach, I'm finding myself rather tempted. Any objections?'

'A little…nostalgia perhaps.' He returned her smile with
an easy one of his own. 'But no objections. Besides, I don't
have any right to any now, have I?'

'Josh, you know perfectly well you'll always have whatever rights you choose. And if you change your mind about
this domestic life you've decided you crave…' Her expression had momentarily turned serious. 'Well, you know
where to find me.'

'Five minutes of luxury in Martin's new Bentley and
you'll have forgotten me completely, and you know it very
well,' Josh chided. 'Take care, Veronica.' From the area
near the bar Josh saw Martin turn as they entered, his regard
somewhat brooding. Gently, he prodded her forward towards the other surgeon. 'Martin's looking a little forlorn.
He's a great guy. You'll have fun with him.'

Veronica sent him a half-mocking backward look and
went towards the plastic surgeon. Josh hesitated for a few
seconds then flicked back the stiff sleeve of his formal shirt,
checked the time, did an abrupt turn and headed back towards the main entrance of the hotel.

He knew that the band was scheduled to play until midnight, with another three hours of dancing and supper still
to come, but it had been a long day and he'd been in
Theatre most of the night, operating on a young woman
who'd been hit by a car on the road outside the hospital.
She'd had multiple abdominal injuries and had lost a lot of
blood. The surgery had been technical and demanding of
his concentration, and he was tired. He considered he'd
fulfilled his duties for the day and, since Veronica had removed from him the obligation to escort her home, he could
think of no reason to stay.

The doorman obviously realised his intent because as
soon as Josh nodded towards him he stepped forward au-
thoritatively with an arm raised to hail the cab Josh needed.
But instead of the black cab he was expecting, the space

where he was waiting was promptly targeted by a tattered and ancient yellow Mini, which veered across two slow-moving but beeping lanes of traffic and limped into the parking area, its flat-looking left front tyre missing his foot by about half an inch.

Josh knew only one person who drove like that, and even if he hadn't recognised the car he'd have known who it was. He signalled to the doorman to delay his search for a cab and moved warily back onto the path and waited, his smile feeling tense and unnatural as the car's dented door was flung open and a very panicked-looking Paige came flying out.

'Have I missed him?' she cried breathlessly, gathering the dark fabric of her long skirt as if to stop herself tripping on it as she hurtled around the back of her car. 'Josh? I know I'm a bit late but, please, tell me he hasn't left already.'

'Ten minutes ago,' he said dryly. 'Paige, you're not a *bit* late. You're ten hours and fifteen minutes late. The ceremony started at eleven.'

'Traffic,' she said vaguely, making a dismissive sort of move with her hands, her lovely eyes wide and so green they almost glowed. 'And how typical of you to keep count of the time,' she added, poking a small pink tongue out at him. 'Years go by but some things never change.'

'Like your tardiness,' he observed, studying the rosy mouth into which her tongue had retreated.

'Ha. Ha.' But she laughed, giving him an enchanting view of perfect white teeth. 'I didn't mean to miss him,' she protested. 'How was he? Happy? I can't believe I missed everything. *Everything.* How ridiculous. How did he look? Nice, I expect. Is he truly happy? Is his Louise nice? Will she be kind to him?'

'David's delirious,' he said quietly. 'And Louise is

lovely and she'll be kind to him always so stop fretting, if that's what you're doing. Hello, Paige.'

'Hello, Josh,' she murmured, holding his arm and going up onto tiptoe to kiss his cheek. Her dark hair swung softly against his face and he found himself briefly surrounded by the delicious, floral scent of her. 'Mmm. You feel good. And you look divine in that tuxedo. I'd almost forgotten how gorgeous you are. It's been ages. I've missed you. I thought we were friends. Why did you never come and see me?'

'You know why.' He returned her sharp look steadily, as always, when Paige was around, aware of the disconcerting feeling of his feet not seeming to quite touch the ground properly. 'You look wonderful,' he declared. Thinner, perhaps, than the last time he'd seen her, and a little pale, some of her old vibrancy dulled a little, but with Paige that still meant that she was more full of life than anyone else he knew. 'I was sorry to hear about your mother. David told me tonight that you've been looking after your father. How is he? How have you been?'

'Dad died six months ago and I'm…getting better,' she said, the last bit coming out very fast. 'I've been a bit depressed. Silly, really. Death is inevitable, we all know that, but there you go.' Her smile was bright but slightly unsteady and he had the impression of concealed pain. 'And you?' she asked. 'What? Tell me everything. Are you still the most eligible bachelor south of the Watford Gap or has some gorgeous woman snatched you up and captured your heart for ever?'

'I'm single and your description of my eligibility suggests you're confusing me with someone else,' he said evenly, taking her small hand in his because he wanted to touch her and it seemed the safest and least personal way to do it and, anyway, he couldn't stop himself. 'I'd be a very bad catch. Come inside, Paige. David's parents are still here. I'm sure they'd love to see you.'

'Oh, but I'm equally sure they wouldn't love that at all,' Paige said lightly, letting him hold her hand although she resisted him by not moving as he wanted her to. 'No, Josh. No. David's parents and I never gelled. They considered me very unsuitable for their son. I wasn't conventional enough, I'm afraid, and definitely not posh enough. Since David's gone, there's really no point in me coming in.' She glanced back to where her car was still obstructing traffic flow around the hotel. 'In fact, I don't want to. I'll just go home.'

He frowned. 'Yorkshire?'

'Malton,' she confirmed.

'Paige, you can't drive all the way back tonight.' He felt the small tugs she was making on his grip but he refused to release her hand. 'It's too far. You'll fall asleep at the wheel and slaughter some innocent family.'

'I'm an excellent driver.'

'No, you're not. You're an appallingly bad driver. You've always been appalling. You don't concentrate properly.' He grinned at her affronted expression then clicked his fingers for her keys. 'Your front tyre's almost flat. I'll take you to a garage and put some air in it. You can stay with me tonight.'

'Am I being offered the use of a spare bedroom?' She'd tilted her head and now she gazed up at him speculatively. 'Or should I be preparing myself for possible seduction attempts?'

'I don't know.' Josh laughed. 'I haven't decided yet.' Holding her gaze, he clicked his fingers again. 'Keys?'

'Keys.' She let them drop into his palm. 'Bossy man.'

He opened the passenger door for her and held it while she climbed in obediently. 'Just out of interest, how does one prepare oneself for possible seduction attempts?'

'One shaves one's legs,' she said smartly, busying herself with moving assorted maps and newspapers and packets of biscuits and jelly beans into the back seat and not looking at him at all. 'Only I've forgotten my razor.'

'I'll buy you a new one,' he said calmly, getting confirmation, if he'd needed it, that her flirtatious banter had merely been meant jokingly from the quick, half-startled, very green look his comment had provoked. 'Just in case.' He shut her door firmly on her suddenly alarmed expression. 'You never can tell.'

CHAPTER TWO

'JOSH, you know I was just teasing.' Paige waited until Josh had slid the driver's seat back as far as it could go and pulled smoothly out into the traffic, before speaking warily. 'Just then. About shaving my legs. You know that, don't you?'

As always with Josh, she was unsure of what he was thinking. David's emotions and motivations had always seemed fairly transparent to her, but not Josh's. Never Josh's. Josh concealed himself in layers of bland, deflecting smiles and pleasant good humour and she'd rarely been granted more than a glimpse of the man beneath those layers. One minute with him tonight had told her that almost three years without seeing him hadn't changed anything about his defensiveness.

'Hmm?' she prompted, when he didn't react. 'Josh…? Tell me you do realise that I wasn't serious.'

But the amused sideways look he sent her made her more nervous. 'I can't believe you're still driving this thing,' he remarked, changing gear, his gaze across the unadorned dash of her beloved car frankly disparaging. 'Listen to it rattle. It's a heap of junk. You must be truly poverty-stricken. Need a loan?'

'No, thank you.' Her father had left her money and the house in Malton, along with a substantial number of investments in what she'd been informed were well-performing funds. The money was meaningless—she would have traded every penny in return for a single extra hour with either of her parents—but at least she hadn't had to worry about trying to earn an income these last months when she'd been too despondent to cope with work. 'This little car is very precious to me. It's reliable and trustworthy and it's my best friend. I love it.'

He laughed. 'And is there anything else you love like that? Any *one* else?'

'Are you asking me if I have a boyfriend?'

He'd stopped for a red traffic light and his look was disconcertingly serious, making her breath catch. 'Is there someone, Paige?'

'My heart is too full with my car to leave me time to think about men,' she announced, worried by her breathlessness. 'I haven't time for lovers and lately I haven't had the energy. Josh, it must be three years since I've seen you, but if feels as if it could have been yesterday. It's as if no time has passed at all. Remember that wonderful afternoon we had in that café? It's like that just happened. It's as if we just left there. Don't you think that's strange?'

The lights changed and he put her car into gear and moved off with a smoothness which struck her as infuriating, given that in six years of driving the Mini she'd never once been able to get it to pull off so evenly.

'Three years isn't such a long time,' he said, signalling to turn right into a garage on the other side of the road.

To Paige it had seemed like an eternity. Three years and the loss of her beloved parents had changed her life completely. In three years she'd gone from being a carefree student, worried only about getting her essays submitted in time, to what felt like a proper grown-up person, aware and fearful of the harsh cruelties that lurked around the corners of her life.

But something that hadn't changed, it seemed, was her reaction to Josh. Being around Josh had always excited her, and she was excited now. 'Tell me what you've been doing,' she urged. 'Are you still at Charing Cross?' she asked, naming the hospital where he'd been working when she'd been living with David. 'Or have you moved? You look very…smooth. I suppose you're terribly high-powered and successful now.'

'I'm still mostly at Charing Cross,' he said heavily, 'although I move between two hospitals these days and I have a private list as well. Whether you'd judge me successful or not would have to depend on your criteria.' He reversed fluidly into the area next to the air pump then levered his tall frame out of the little car. 'When's the last time you checked the pressures?'

Paige tried to think. 'The man at the garage…used to do it,' she said finally. 'When I got petrol. I think. Only I haven't driven a lot lately so I haven't needed petrol.'

He didn't say anything but she was aware of the vaguely impatient brush of his gaze across her face before he shut the door. She heard the hissing sounds of him checking air pressure and adding air to the tyre he'd told her looked flat. When he moved to the rear tyre on that side she lowered her window and swivelled around in her seat, leaning out and watching him, smiling at the incongruous picture of Josh, so impossibly handsome in his tuxedo and snowy shirt, crouched beside her dusty little car frowning in concentration over the tyre pressure gauge.

He saw her looking at him and smiled at her, then moved around behind the car to the tyres over the other side. When he'd finished he went towards the shop, and when he came back he had a plastic bag for her.

'I'm afraid I don't know much about shaving legs but this one says it's designed especially for *ladies*,' he said evenly when she opened the bag and peered inside.

'I'm not a lady, I'm a woman,' she said automatically, aware of a flutter in her chest starting as she studied the contents of the packet. 'Josh—'

'Paige.' He smiled again as he started her car then pulled out of the garage forecourt. 'Just in case.'

'I can see you've become a shameless flirt,' she told him, dazzled by him. Since it was years since anyone had flirted with her, let alone someone as appealing as Josh, she wasn't sure how best to deal with it. 'David always said you were but you never used to be with me. Were you too worried I'd take you seriously? Still, it's very flattering to be given a glimpse of the famous charm treatment. Will it continue, do you think? Or are you beginning to be bored already?'

'Do you ever ask one question at a time?'

'Perhaps if you just once answered one properly…'

'I didn't know my charm treatment was famous.'

'David's words,' she told him.

They were driving around Marble Arch now, and although there was a big red bus next to them, making a lot of noise, she still thought she heard Josh sigh. 'David has always exaggerated things like that, Paige. Things to do with me and women. He gets vicarious enjoyment out of pretending I have a wildly adventurous sex life.'

She smiled as they drove along. 'If you say so, Josh.' David did have a tendency to embellish stories to make them more entertaining, but privately Paige doubted whether David had exaggerated that much when it had come to Josh. Given how attractive Josh was, David's tales of his friend's conquests seemed entirely feasible.

He turned off the main road, then slowed, stopped and reversed fluidly into a space, a space so small that Paige, yet to master the delicate science of parking, wouldn't have even dreamed of trying, despite the smallness of the Mini. They were outside a row of expensive-looking terraces close to Holland Park in West London. Paige knew the area vaguely because the flat she'd shared with David had been in Turnham Green, a short distance further west, and she'd regularly caught a bus which had passed by the end of the street.

It suddenly struck her as strange that in all her time of living with David this was the first time she'd visited Josh's home. She climbed quickly out of the car, peered up at the building then let out a long whistle. 'Oh, my goodness!' she exclaimed. 'If you live here then you've done extremely well for yourself, Dr Allard.'

'*Mr* Allard,' he corrected. He'd come around to her side and now he tapped her nose. 'As a surgeon, I'm a Mister, Miss Connolly.'

'Ms Connolly,' Paige said, wrinkling her nose. 'As a liberated woman, I'm a Ms, Mr Allard. So, do you?'

'Do I what?'

'Live here?'

'Most of the time.'

'When you're not with your mistresses,' she supplied, skipping after him towards the brass-handled door he was unlocking.

'I don't have mistresses.' He flicked a switch just inside the door, which illuminated an open glass door and a long hall, and stood back for her to precede him inside. 'I'm not married.'

'Girlfriends, then,' she said vaguely. She tipped her head back and blinked, peering up at the ornately plastered ceiling and its elaborate chandelier. 'Wow! This is impressive.' The luxuriously thick carpet her feet had sunk into felt about six inches thick. 'I had no idea surgeons were paid this much. So, are you massively wealthy, then, Josh?'

'That's a very impolite question.' But he looked more amused than offended. He dropped his keys onto the antique-looking desk inside the main room with a carelessness that suggested its value left him unmoved.

'The place is an anachronism,' he declared, heading towards a broad staircase. 'My grandfather lived here most of his life, and I inherited part of it and bought the rest. It needs to be modernised but I've never mustered the energy to organise it. Make yourself at home. The kitchen's up on the next level if you want a drink and there are bathrooms about the place. Bedrooms and the study are on the two top floors. I just want to get this suit off.'

Paige wandered around interestedly, opening doors here and there and exploring the lower two floors, looking in vain for any evidence that this imposing yet impersonal residence could be Josh's home.

'Either you are obsessively tidy or you have an extraordinarily fussy cleaner,' she told him, when she heard his footsteps behind her as she opened door after door of immaculate kitchen cupboards.

'I'm obsessively tidy *and* I have a fussy cleaner. Paige…?'

'Teabags.' She turned around with a smile that faltered when she saw that he'd exchanged his formal suit for a pair of worn, pale jeans which clung lovingly in all the right places and a cream jersey which filled her with the immediate and alarming urge to bury her face against him. 'And I thought the suit was impressive,' she said thickly. 'I expect you've been told this a million times, Josh, but you are hopelessly devastating. Forgive me if I swoon on you, won't you? My legs have gone quite weak. Do you have chamomile?'

'I suspect the choice is Ceylon or Indian.' Frowning slightly, he went for the cupboard furthest from her above the refrigerator. 'No, make that Chinese as well. And you're a shameless liar, Paige Connolly. You've never swooned over any male. You have a briskly practical air about you when it comes to us poor men.'

'You only think that because you let my chatter deceive you,' she countered. 'What you haven't understood is that I talk far more when I'm nervous than when I'm not.'

'And do I make you nervous?'

'Oh, of course.' She beamed. 'Terribly nervous. And excited. You always have. Nothing herbal, then?'

'Only normal teas,' he told her, lifting out the packets so she could see them. 'Why would you be nervous with me?'

'You've always been rather too tempting when I haven't wanted to be tempted,' she revealed. 'Ceylon, please.'

'Paige, David's married.' He brought down the tea, then closed the cupboard. 'Any reason for not being tempted is gone.'

'I still don't want to be,' she countered firmly. Aware that her hands had started to tremble, she put them behind her back. 'My life is far too complicated already at present, thank you, without adding you to the mix.' She knew he was teasing her again, but even when teasing he had the power to make her breathless. 'Shall I make the tea or are you still planning to do it yourself?'

'I'll do it,' he said evenly, the gleam in his narrowed gaze as it skimmed her confirmed her impression that he'd merely been playing with her. 'Just sit and look beautiful.' He indicated a table with four stools on the other side of the room. 'Are you hungry? Shall I make you an omelette?'

'I ate fast food on the motorway.' Paige sat, wondering how best to make herself look beautiful when she knew the make-up she'd applied for the wedding had to be long gone and her hair, so badly in need of a good cut, was curling around her shoulders in what felt like utter disarray. 'I don't want food. Tell me about the wedding.'

'It was just a normal wedding. Church, photos, speeches, food—you know the sort of thing. There weren't any surprises.'

'What did Louise wear?'

'Long white dress,' he told her with a vagueness that struck her as so male it made her smile. 'A veil thing.'

'And the bridesmaids?'

'Pink.' He was putting the water on to boil but then he hesitated. 'Or yellow.'

On the invitation he'd sent her David had written that Josh was to be best man. 'Were any of the bridesmaids terribly beautiful?' she asked dreamily, thinking about the traditional wedding pairings.

'I don't know.' His glance was more knowing than she'd have liked it to be and goose-bumps rose fleetingly across her arms. 'I didn't notice.'

'Did you go alone?'

'No.'

'Then why were you alone when I saw you?'

'My partner decided to go home with someone else.' He folded his arms, his expression enigmatic. 'Is this twenty questions?'

'Surely I've gone past twenty,' she said lightly. 'Come on, Josh. Spill the beans. I can't believe she ditched you, with you looking the way you did tonight.'

'I was definitely ditched.' But he didn't appear particularly bothered by the fact. 'Do you remember Martin Stanton?'

'Martin? Of course I remember Martin. He's lovely. But hardly in your league, Josh. Surely she didn't chuck you over for Martin?'

'He offered her a ride in his new Bentley,' he said dryly. 'Veronica seemed quite taken by the idea.'

'Oh, poor Josh.' But since he didn't look remotely upset, even seemed, perhaps, amused by her pity, she laughed. 'You're so callous, you horrible man. I bet you set it up. I take it you're not mortally wounded?'

'I'll survive.' He smiled at her. 'Milk or lemon?'

'Milk.' She waited for him to disconnect the kettle from its power supply. 'What about the speeches? How were they?'

He added a splash of the boiling water to a very elegant-looking teapot then swirled it around and discarded it. 'Normal speeches,' he told her, adding spoons of tea to the pot. 'I didn't take notes.'

'But weren't you best man?'

'I told a few stories. People laughed kindly in the right places.'

'Was it romantic? Do they seem very much in love?'

'I've never thought of weddings as being especially romantic but they do seem to be in love, yes.' He brought the tea to the table where she sat, together with two finely painted china cups with matching saucers. 'Jealous?'

'Of course not.' She sent him a startled look. 'What a silly thing to say. I want David to be happy.'

'It's not silly. You were in love with him yourself once.'

'I wasn't in love with him.'

'Of course you were.'

'Of course I *wasn't*.' Resisting the uncouth urge to turn up her teacup to check what she was sure would be a very prestigious label, Paige took the strainer he offered her and poured her tea. 'At least not for very long. I prefer mine very weak,' she explained, when the liquid came out barely coloured. 'You, too, or will you wait?'

'Another minute or two,' he said heavily. 'Paige, you lived with David almost two years. He told me tonight that you weren't romantically involved all that time, but you're not the sort of person who'd spend so long with someone lightly. Particularly not when it was obvious he was in love with you. Why did you stay if you didn't return his feelings?'

Paige added a cube of sugar to her tea and then stirred it slowly, remembering. 'I did in the beginning,' she admitted cautiously. 'At least I thought I did at the time. But I was young, only two years out of school, remember, and in London, away from my parents for the first time. David was my first boyfriend. I wasn't old enough to understand my feelings properly.'

She tilted her head and smiled faintly at Josh's frown as he seemed to be trying to work that out. 'I hope you're wrong about David being in love with me,' she added sincerely. 'I didn't think he was. Not after the first few months or so.'

She'd met David through a fellow student who'd worked weekends as a nurse at the general practice where David had worked. He'd asked her out and they'd got on very well. They'd had similar interests—they'd liked the same books and he'd loved art and going to see films the same way she'd done—and she'd loved his lively, self-deprecating sense of humour. They'd had a wonderful time together.

When the owner of the flat she'd been sharing with two friends had given notice of a large rent increase, moving in with David, as he'd suggested, had seemed a natural progression of their relationship.

'I'm still very fond of him,' she said huskily. 'But we both realised quite quickly that being a couple wasn't going to work out. Living together was completely different to just going out. Little things started bothering him. Me running a couple of minutes late would drive him crazy.' She saw Josh's mouth quirk at that, and she narrowed her eyes at him. 'Like it does you,' she said firmly. 'I'm never deliberately late. Never. In fact, I hate it. I just… Things happen to stop me getting to places on time.'

'Things that don't happen to other people,' he pointed out. 'It's been years since I was late for anything.'

Paige wrinkled her nose at him. 'It must be nice, being so superior.'

He laughed. 'So David was a stickler for punctuality?'

'Terrible,' she confirmed. 'Also, he used to fret I was going to bankrupt myself. There was this lovely flower stall

at the tube station but David used to throw his hands up in
the air whenever I bought any. He thought it was silly to
buy flowers just because of their lovely smell when I only
had my grant and a little bit of money from my parents. It
was obvious pretty soon that we weren't suited.'

So she'd moved her things out of David's room and into
the flat's other bedroom. At first she'd meant to leave al-
together but he'd persuaded her to stay. He'd needed the
rent, he'd insisted. Privately she'd doubted that. He'd just
been being kind, she'd decided, and that had increased her
affection for him and she'd allowed herself to be convinced.

Surprising both of them, she suspected, just sharing his
home had worked out well. In between her studies she'd
cooked for him and done the major and smaller cleaning
chores David had never seemed to realise needed doing.
'In those two years David went out with other women,
Josh.'

But Josh was frowning at her. 'Did you meet any?'

'One or two, I think.' Now Paige frowned, trying to
think, wondering if her memory was deceiving her on that.
'I vaguely remember one, I think.'

'Neither of you even hinted you weren't a couple.'

'I—I…' She trailed off, knowing he'd caught her there.
'For myself I didn't mention it deliberately,' she said flatly.
'I knew you didn't realise but I didn't think it was my place
to tell you. I'm sure he's more confident now, but in those
days David was sensitive about what you—' She broke off,
amending her words to, 'About what his friends thought.
He liked people thinking we were living together. I felt that
it was up to him to tell you about us if that was what he
wanted.'

She returning his steady gaze unflinchingly. 'Besides, it
wasn't as if you needed to know. I would never have agreed
to go out with…any of David's friends. Even if he didn't

want me himself, David wouldn't have liked that. And I wouldn't have wanted to hurt him.'

The darkening of his eyes told her he understood what she was saying. 'I remember the first time he introduced you to me,' he said gruffly. 'He kept his arm around you the whole afternoon. Even when he had to go to the bar he didn't take his eyes off you.'

'We'd just started going out.' Paige remembered the afternoon vividly. David had explained that Josh had been working a busy one-in-two rotation as a surgical registrar at Charing Cross, and one Sunday afternoon he'd taken her to meet him at a pub close to his hospital in Hammersmith.

She'd been painfully nervous. She'd been young and unsure of herself and David had been so excited about her meeting his friend she'd been worried she wouldn't achieve Josh's approval. It had been very clear that achieving Josh's approval had been important to David.

From the things David had told her about his friend—Josh's academic achievements at school and then at university where he'd always been among the top in his classes, and his sporting prowess, including the fact he'd represented his university at both cricket and rugby—she'd expected either a snobbish, intellectual type or an athletic, macho male who'd quickly sum her up and dismiss her as not being good enough for his friend.

But instead there was Josh. Impossibly, knee-weakeningly handsome but at the same time smiling and friendly Josh. If she hadn't been with David she might have fallen in love with him then and there, she realised immediately. He teased her and he made her laugh, and the afternoon was wonderful.

The three of them met often after that for the first eighteen months of the time she was living at David's. There were weekends away together in the country, a lot of weddings and casual meetings with other friends.

Six months before she left London they met once alone. It was a week before David's birthday and Josh had offered to help with the arrangements for the surprise party she was planning. He'd been on call for the weekend and had been rostered a free Monday afternoon so they met for a late lunch to talk about the party.

Only once they had the details sorted, she didn't leave. They talked and laughed in the café all afternoon and into the night and for hours and hours until the impatient staff finally threw them out after midnight.

For Paige, who until then had been conscious of David's watchfulness when Josh was about and painfully aware of how it would hurt him if she revealed how much she craved the other man's company, the private hours alone with Josh were exhilarating. It was as if she was bursting with things to tell him, experiences to share and laugh about, along with an urgency to know more about him and to understand him.

But after a cold, sleepless night she knew that the blissful rapport of that day could never be repeated. It was too dangerous. Josh hadn't touched her that day. He hadn't kissed her or invited her to his home, yet she knew, from how he'd looked at her and from the helpless excitement she'd felt in response, that they were close to going to bed together.

She didn't kid herself that he was developing any emotional attachment for her—David's tales of what he saw as Josh's enviably exciting love life meant she was pre-warned about how casually Josh could treat sex—but she knew he wanted her.

As she wanted him. Only sex wouldn't be enough for her so she knew she'd be hurt. Perhaps as much as David would be hurt by what she was sure he'd see—despite their own relationship being one of friendship now—as being her desertion of him for his best friend.

So she was sensible. She and Josh had arranged to meet the following evening—ostensibly to discuss more party plans, although she knew he knew as well as she did that that was an excuse—but instead she called him the next morning at his hospital and gave him a carefully rehearsed little speech about how she had David's party arranged now and how any more discussion would be unnecessary.

His calm acceptance of her words told her that he, too, had been having doubts and that was the end of it. He didn't come to David's birthday party. When she asked a few days later, David revealed that Josh had called him to apologise and that he'd been on call and had been unable to make it.

Six months or so later, her mother died. Paige left London and returned to Yorkshire to live. That day in the café had been the last time she'd seen Josh until tonight. 'You missed a great party,' she told him, remembering. 'David's surprise birthday that year. It went on until lunchtime on the Sunday.'

'He told me you made him a wonderful cake.'

'"Wonderful" is a terrible exaggeration,' she said, smiling at the generosity of David's description. 'I baked it into a shape like a hospital bed. I made a marzipan doctor to look like David to sit on the top, but he came out looking more like a rabbit. As I'd put a green cover on the bed people thought the whole thing was a rabbit on a lawn. No one really understood.'

Having finished her second cup of tea, she put her cup and the pot aside. 'But they were polite and they ate it. Enough of me,' she finished crisply. 'Tell me what you've been up to all this time.'

'Working.' He lifted one broad shoulder with an air of disinterest, as if he didn't consider the time had counted at all. 'It doesn't seem like much else. What are you going to do with yourself now?'

'I don't know,' she admitted slowly with a sigh, aware

that he'd deliberately changed the subject back to her but since his question seemed sincere it would have felt rude not to answer. 'My GP tells me I need a holiday. He's insisting I go somewhere sunny and lie on a beach for a month.'

'You don't sound keen.'

'I don't want to go away. What I need is to get back to a normal sort of life again. The first step should be to find a job.'

'Have you been working in Yorkshire?'

'Looking after Dad was a full-time responsibility. And after Mum died so suddenly there was only me to do it. He had a big stroke about five years ago and he needed lots of help. He could manage a few steps with support but for the most part he found it easier to stay in his wheelchair. Last year he had another stroke. He lost his speech and the movement down one side, and after that he was virtually confined to the house.'

'He didn't want to go into a hospital?'

'Oh, I couldn't have suggested it.' His doctors had mentioned the idea but Paige had found the thought horrifying. Her father would have hated it. As it was, he'd hated being dependent on her, but to have had to rely on strangers… 'If I'd had a family of my own or been in full-time work it probably would have had to have been different,' she said huskily. 'But as I had no other obligations I was free to be there for him. And I loved being there. These last few years were very precious. He was a wonderful man.'

'Paige…?' Her face had become pale as she'd spoken about her father, and she looked wistful and sad. Josh worried for her. His concern and his fondness for her were far stronger than the reservations he'd had about needing time to reconsider what exactly it was that he wanted now in the wake of David's revelations at the wedding. 'Why don't you stay with me for a while?'

She blinked at him. 'Why?'

'You said you've been depressed. From the little you've told me, that's hardly surprising. Your doctor's probably right when he says you need a holiday, but you don't have to go abroad. Give yourself some time to recuperate a little before you plunge into work. Stay in London. And if you're determined to find a job, look here. There has to be more work in London than in Malton.'

Paige felt her brow furrowing. 'Josh, that's very kind of you. But I couldn't possibly impose—'

'I'm not being kind, Paige.' He still spoke quietly but, she thought, more firmly now. 'You won't be an imposition. You're like a feather. You take up no room at all. You're tired and pale and you've lost too much weight. You're brittle. Fragile. Let me look after you.'

But still she frowned. 'Why are you offering this?'

'Aren't we friends?'

His expression was shadowed and utterly unreadable and she was confused. 'I'd like to think we are, but, still, you hardly know me,' she said faintly.

'Of course I know you.' Josh's smile was gentle now. 'Are you hesitating out of politeness or are you genuinely not interested?'

'I'm tempted,' she admitted. 'I think.' The house had seemed terribly lonely with just her there in it, but she still couldn't bear the thought of selling it. And while she didn't think a holiday would do anything to help distract her from her grief, the idea of a little time away from the house while she sorted out her life was appealing. 'Are you sure, Josh?'

'I wouldn't suggest it if I wasn't.' He stood. 'It's after midnight and you've had a long drive. Sleep on it, Paige. There's no hurry. Let me know when you've decided.' He held out a hand for her. 'I'll show you your room.'

She bent to retrieve the bag he'd brought in, smiling when she caught sight of the smaller package containing the shaver he'd brought for her. 'So I'm not about to be seduced, then?'

'Not tonight.' He spoke easily, his warm arm coming around her back as he guided her towards the stairs. 'I had a late night last night and you're too tired. Another time, when we've more energy.'

Paige blinked up at him, not sure now whether to continue treating his teasing as a joke or not. 'I think it's only fair to warn you,' she said huskily, 'that if your invitation to stay is part of some devious plot you're evolving to get me into bed, you probably needn't bother.'

'Because the plot won't succeed?'

'I'm not robust enough to be able to cope with sexual shenanigans right now,' she said honestly, meeting his dark inspection when they paused outside a cream door at the top of the stairs with a calm she was far from feeling. 'But if I should feel that way inclined in the future then you'll only have to ask, Josh. We both know I'd find you utterly irresistible.'

The warm hand holding hers tightened fractionally. 'Do you think it's safe to be so forthright, Paige?'

'I try to be honest.' Her mouth had gone very dry. 'If I were to stay with you then I think it's important that we both understand exactly where we stand.' She went up on tiptoe and kissed his cheek. 'Goodnight, darling Josh. Thank you so much. See you tomorrow.'

CHAPTER THREE

JOSH was up at his usual time of six. He changed into his running gear and headed downstairs, but when he opened the front door and saw that Paige's ghastly yellow Mini was gone he went back inside. There was a note waiting for him on the table in the kitchen, saying she'd woken early and was making an early start to her trip home to Yorkshire. 'I'll be in touch,' she'd written unhelpfully, before signing herself with a huge 'P' and adding a sprinkling of criss-cross kisses.

He studied the kisses thoughtfully and found himself still thinking about them when he returned from his run around Holland Park thirty minutes later.

Josh wasn't used to feeling disarmed. He was used to being effortlessly in command of both his emotions and his relationships with women, but where Paige was concerned he'd never quite managed to muster control of either. The first time he'd met her she'd unsettled him thoroughly and her tendency to do that had never grown any less dramatic. The sensation wasn't any more comfortable now than it had been three years before.

When she'd been with David, his options had been clear in that they'd been non-existent. The fact that he'd found her utterly desirable had been irrelevant. He'd kept his hands off her because morally and rationally it had been the only thing he could do.

But now David was married and both he and Paige were unattached. So now that left him…where?

Throwing his discarded running gear into the laundry box, he stepped beneath his shower and adjusted the water to strong lukewarm. He wasn't sure, he admitted. Just as he was rarely sure of anything with Paige. He didn't regret his invitation because if she was as in need of a refuge as she seemed then he wanted to offer her that. But if she did accept his offer, there was no way he could kid himself that she was just going to be an ordinary house guest. Not when his senses reacted to her now as violently as they'd ever done. Since she'd made it clear that she wasn't ready to share his bed, having her in his home and sharing his life, however superficially, wasn't going to be easy.

The roster he worked at the hospital involved being on call only one weekend in four but he routinely called into the wards for early ward rounds on Saturdays and Sundays to check on the progress of his patients.

'No problems with any of yours, Josh.' Bunty, his main ward's charge nurse greeted him with a welcoming beam when he walked in. 'Intensive Care tell me that Emma McDermott, the poor hit-and-run lass you operated on Friday night, is doing very well and they might send her to us later today if you agree.'

Josh nodded. 'I'll check on her after we've been around here.'

The nurse collected her big ward notebook but instead of bustling off ahead of him down the ward as he was expecting, she leaned over the nursing station and fluttered her eyelashes at him. 'I thought you'd be in late this morning, considering your big night last night. How was the wedding?'

'Fine.'

'And what about Louise's chief bridesmaid?'

'I didn't get a chance to speak to her.' He eyed her disappointed expression dispassionately. 'Cut it out, Bunty.'

'So who was the girl in the yellow Mini?'

Josh wondered why he hadn't been expecting that. Because David had trained at the hospital and still worked close by, and because Louise was a nurse on the children's ward, there'd been a heavy contingent of hospital staff at the wedding, including the bridesmaid Bunty seemed determined to matchmake him with. He should have known that word of anything he did would leak back to Bunty because Bunty prided herself on keeping up with all gossip. 'Bunty—'

'One of the nurses from upstairs told me she looked like a beautiful doll. She said she came and picked you up from the hotel and you jumped right in and drove away with her.'

'She didn't exactly pick me up,' Josh said heavily. 'The truth is she nearly ran over my foot—'

But Bunty clearly had no interest in the truth. 'Josh, you told me you weren't seeing anyone at present,' she declared. 'I've half the unmarried nurses on my staff after you—probably a good number of the married ones as well—yet you go off chasing some unknown young thing in a yellow Mini! What am I to tell them all?'

'I'm not—'

'Interested in any of my staff,' she finished with another one of her motherly beams. 'Well, Josh, you're just going to have to get interested, you know you are. It's time you married and I'm going to help you. I've found wives for three horrible sons and one ugly nephew so I'm not about to give up on you. You might think you like being a bachelor, but that's only because you don't understand how wonderful marriage is for a man. You should have flirted with Catherine. She's perfect for you.'

'Remind me again next wedding,' he relented. Bunty meant well, he knew, even if he didn't appreciate her efforts. 'Come on now, Bunty. Let's have some action. Work action. How's Mr Parsons's wound?'

'We've taken the dressings down for you to see.'

Josh was pleased with the wound. Ted Parsons was an

elderly man under his care who'd been admitted ten days earlier critically ill with abdominal pain, septicaemia and shock. His abdomen had been rigid to touch and when Josh had operated and opened it he'd discovered the septicaemia had been caused by a neglected and perforated appendix. Mr Parsons's post-op progress had been good considering how ill he'd been but, not surprisingly considering the extent of his inflammation, he'd developed a wound infection.

'Much, much better,' Josh said approvingly when he'd finished his examination. 'Well done. Take out the last of those stitches today,' he told Bunty, indicating the ones he meant, 'and a simple dry dressing for a few days.'

'Mr Parsons has been walking well,' his nurse contributed quietly. 'He's been up and about the floor these past two days, and he's already been off to church this morning.'

Josh smiled. 'Then how would you feel about going home tomorrow, Mr Parsons?'

'Tomorrow?' His patient had clearly been hoping for something like that since, apart from his exposed abdomen, he was fully dressed in a neat suit and tie rather than his pyjamas. 'I'd like that,' the eighty-nine-year-old admitted. 'Not that my care here hasn't been good, mind,' he added, his eyes twinkling towards Bunty. 'But a soul could get too used to being looked after, and I do want to maintain my independence.'

'Perfectly understandable,' responded Josh with a grin. He hoped that if he reached the same age his own concerns would be similar. 'We'll liaise with your GP to have a nurse check your wound in a few days and I'll call in myself in a week or so to save you coming up to the clinic. If you have any problems don't hesitate to ring the ward or my secretary.'

'You've all been very kind,' Mr Parsons said, putting out his hand. 'Thank you again, Mr Allard.'

'My pleasure,' Josh said sincerely, pleased with the strength of the older man's grip when he shook his hand. 'Will you need help with transport home or will Evelyn be able to fetch you?'

'She'll be happy to,' Mr Parsons told him, referring to one of his daughters. Josh knew from speaking with Evelyn that she lived closer to her father than his other three children.

'She'll be surprised when I tell her.' The older man chuckled. 'She was expecting to take me out of here in a coffin.'

'I had a few thoughts that way myself,' Josh admitted with a smile, moving to the basin beside the bed to wash his hands. 'Happily, you've proven us both wrong. I'll see you tomorrow morning before you leave.'

After finishing on the main surgical wards, he called into the intensive care unit where his young patient from Friday night was doing well. 'We took her tube out last night and she's awake and breathing well,' the registrar on the unit for the weekend told him. 'The on-call team were in last night to see her and they're pleased with her progress.' He showed Josh through the previous day's blood results and fluid balance chart. 'The orthopaedic mob have been in and there're no problems with the leg. If you're happy with her abdomen we'll send her to a surgical ward later today.'

'Good,' Josh agreed, as they approached the bed. 'Morning, Emma.' He'd met his patient's boyfriend after the surgery and he nodded a greeting. 'I'm Josh Allard,' he told his patient. 'You won't remember me but I operated on you Friday night. How are you feeling?'

'Bruised and battered,' the young woman said huskily. 'Like I've been run over by a van, I suppose.' She and her boyfriend exchanged wry looks. 'I don't remember anything about the accident,' she added. 'But I know I've got a broken leg and you've taken out my kidney.'

'One kidney plus your spleen,' he confirmed. 'I'm afraid they were too crushed to save.'

'What does it all mean?'

'Your remaining kidney's functioning well,' he reassured her. 'You won't miss the other.' He explained the spleen's role in filtering the blood and fighting infection. 'Last night one of the nurses here vaccinated you against a bacterium which can cause problems when you don't have a spleen. You'll need to ensure that doctors looking after you in the future know about the operation.'

'She won't be needing that dialysis thing, then, Doctor?' Her boyfriend looked unsure. 'Only one of the students on our course has to be on that for hours every other day and we were wondering.'

'Emma won't be needing dialysis at all,' Josh said firmly. 'That's something that's only needed when neither kidney functions. One healthy kidney is more than enough to live a normal life.'

He examined Emma's abdomen. 'This feels fine,' he told her. His main incision was still covered by a sterile dressing but the area around it was soft and he could hear bowel sounds. 'Your tummy's making excellent progress.' He was pleased by how rapidly her bowel sounds had returned. 'The nurses will take that tube out of your nose and you can start drinking today. Start with sips of water and build up over the day if you don't feel sick.'

'I'd kill for a cup of tea.'

'After lunch if you're feeling well,' he promised. 'This drain can come out this morning,' he told her nurse, indicating the tube he meant, 'along with the nasogastric and central lines. The other two drains should stay in until I say they're to be removed and we'll stick to peripheral lines on the ward. Continue heparin and antibiotics but the urine and drainage measurements can be tailed back to four-hourly once she's transferred.'

The registrar came with him back towards the desk, where Josh stopped to write his assessment into Emma McDermott's notes. 'Any news on the driver?' asked Josh.

'The police are still looking.' The other doctor shrugged. 'We heard on the radio that they've got witnesses, saying it was a white van, but obviously that doesn't narrow it down too much. You know she was on a pedestrian crossing just near here.'

'I heard that.' Josh had caught a report of the incident on the radio the day before. 'Have her parents been found?'

'Flying in this morning from Florida,' the registrar told him. 'The police tracked them down via their rental car.'

'If they arrive before you send her to the ward, bleep me,' Josh told him. 'They'll be anxious. I'm happy to come and explain things to them. The ward staff will contact me if they arrive later.'

From the unit he went to his office. Normally on Sundays he spent the mornings and early afternoons catching up on the paperwork he rarely had time to deal with during the week, but for once he found himself restless.

He worked for an hour or so but his concentration kept lapsing. After pacing the room, he picked up a file at random from the pile collected on his desk and flicked through it, trying to keep himself focused, but his attention drifted again and finally, with a frustrated sigh, he acknowledged there was little point in continuing.

He knew what his problem was. But resigning himself to writing off the rest of the day as unproductive wasn't as startling an admission for him as resigning himself to spending the day contemplating Paige and what her reappearance meant for him.

He checked with Intensive Care and found that Emma McDermott's parents had just arrived. Promising to be along in a few minutes, he punched out the code for an outside line then called one of his golf partners. He wouldn't spend the afternoon brooding about an enchanting face, a gorgeous body and an impossibly disordered mind, he decided. He'd spend it usefully on the golf course.

He didn't hear from Paige until Tuesday night of the following week when she called, waking him from deep sleep. 'If your invitation is still open then I'd like to accept it,' she announced without preamble or bothering to introduce herself. 'So, is it, Josh? Or have you wisely withdrawn it and do you never want to hear from me again?'

'Yes. No. Of course not.' The wave of pleasure he felt at hearing from her pushed the reservations he'd been harbouring into the background. 'When are you coming?'

'Now. I've decided. I'm all packed.'

Josh fumbled for the lamp beside his bed then checked his watch. 'It's one-thirty in the morning.'

'Meaning the M1 should be quiet. I might be there by eight. Nine perhaps. Eleven at the latest. Will you be there?'

'I leave for work at seven. I'll leave the outside door unlocked and I'll bury the key to the inside door in the geranium just inside.' But he was worried now about her driving late at night. 'Wouldn't it be safer to sleep now and get a fresh start in the morning?'

'I'm wide awake,' she declared. 'I had a nap this afternoon. Besides, I haven't slept properly in months. See you soon. Bye, Josh.'

'Paige, drive carefully—'

But she'd hung up and he was left holding a dead receiver. Seconds after he'd replaced it the phone rang again.

'Josh, I'm really, really sorry,' Paige said breathlessly when he answered. 'You're right. It is one-thirty in the morning. I wasn't thinking properly. Just because I can't sleep, it doesn't mean the rest of the world can't. I must have woken you. I'm so sorry. I expect you've got a terribly busy day tomorrow and I've just broken your sleep. I didn't mean to be inconsiderate. I'm just…excited about things. Will you be able to get back to sleep again?'

'I'm going to try,' he said evenly. 'Goodnight, Paige.'

'Goodnight, darling Josh. Sleep well.'

Josh was on call for all general surgical admissions to the hospital the next day, as well as scheduled to be in Theatres all morning. From time to time between his cases he tried ringing Paige from one of the telephones in Theatre, but he kept getting his own voice and the stilted-sounding message he'd recorded on his answering machine.

Seconds after removing his gloves after his last case, his registrar called him to ask for help with a fifty-five-year-old woman the younger man had been asked to see by one of the casualty officers. 'Mr Allard, I think we're going to have to operate immediately.'

Josh ran to Casualty. A flushed, frail, dark-haired woman was lying rigidly still on a trolley in the resuscitation area of the department. Josh could see that her fingers had blanched white where they gripped the side rails of the bed and her face was strained and creased with pain.

'Mrs Lacy, I'm Josh Allard,' he said briskly. He glanced quickly through the abdominal and chest X-rays the casualty officer had organised earlier then took his patient's hand, registering the heat and the clamminess of her skin, along with the feeble and rapid fluttering of her pulse beneath his fingers. 'I'm the on-call surgeon here for today. Mr Chang, my registrar, has just been telling me he thinks you need an operation today.'

'Anything,' his patient gasped. 'Anything, Doctor, for the pain.'

Josh lifted Mrs Lacy's gown and gently examined her rigid abdomen. He raised his brows at his registrar and the other doctor nodded.

'The nurses are organising morphine,' he explained to Josh. 'I've given Mrs Lacy her first dose of antibiotics and that's the third bag of fluid going in now. I've cross-matched four units of blood and they'll be ready in fifteen minutes.'

Josh nodded but since Mrs Lacy was obviously severely dehydrated he released the control wheel regulating the flow through the line so that it moved freely. He nodded for the casualty nurse to prepare a replacement for when that finished. He took his stethoscope out of the pocket of his white coat, bent over Mrs Lacy and listened to her abdomen, not surprised, after examining her, that he could hear none of the normal signs of bowel activity.

William had given him a brief history on the telephone but he needed to confirm the details for himself. 'How long have you been having pain?' he asked.

'Four days,' Mrs Lacy said faintly. 'Just on and off at first and a lot of vomiting. I thought—' She gasped a little and broke off, then collected herself again. 'I thought it was colic,' she explained jerkily. 'From something I'd eaten. But then last night…it's been all the time. I don't dare move. I didn't want to come to hospital but…my neighbour came to see me and she insisted. She called an ambulance.'

'She did the right thing.' Without surgery, if he was right about the cause of her pain, she could have been dead within twenty-four hours. The X-rays, the rigidity of her abdomen, her fever and her state of shock suggested that her bowel obstruction had advanced to the state where the bowel was dead or close to it. The result of that was invariably overwhelming septicaemia and death.

Two nurses hurried in, bearing a kidney dish containing the morphine and anti-nausea medication William had ordered, and Josh moved out of their way to allow them to administer both. 'We're giving you morphine now, which should dull the pain,' he told Mrs Lacy. 'We're going to need to operate immediately.'

'Cancer?' she gasped.

'That is a possibility,' he conceded frankly. 'Until I look I won't know for sure because there are many benign causes of this sort of problem as well. All I can tell from examining you and from looking at your X-rays is that you need urgent surgery. We can't wait. All right?'

'Yes, fine.' She nodded, then closed her eyes. 'I'm feeling a bit dizzy now. Is that…?'

'The morphine,' he confirmed. 'That means it's taking effect now. Good.' Leaving William and the casualty nurses to finalise the necessary details of Mrs Lacy's urgent admission and transfer, Josh returned to Theatres to warn the duty staff there, along with the rostered duty anaesthetist, about their emergency.

Operating quickly in cases of bowel obstruction wasn't necessarily ideal—anaesthetists preferred to wait until patients had had several hours of fluid replacement and resuscitation—but Josh was sure in this case that it was too dangerous to wait.

Once Mrs Lacy was anaesthetised in the operating theatre Josh swabbed the skin of her abdomen and draped her with sterile guards, leaving only the operating field exposed. William finished scrubbing and gowning and joined him on the opposite side of the operating table as he began his incision.

The problem was clear within minutes. A large loop of intestine had twisted around what looked like a tumour, and the pressure build-up and swelling meant the bowel's blood supply had been cut off and that had led to gangrene. Josh removed the dead and dying tissue, along with the tumour, and smoothly rejoined the two healthy ends left behind.

'What do you think, Josh?' the scrub nurse who'd been assisting them asked as they were preparing to close the abdomen at the end of the operation.

'Her chances are good,' Josh conceded. 'The tumour

looked contained and there were no signs of liver or lymph-node involvement.' Cancer of the bowel had a good prognosis in the early stages. Even when the original tumour had grown large enough to obstruct the bowel, if there was no evidence of spread then the chance of the surgery he'd just performed having cured Mrs Lacy was still high. 'We'll know for sure once the lab's had a chance to look at the tissue.' He raised his brows over his mask at his anaesthetist. 'ICU, Ned?'

'Twenty-four hours at least,' the anaesthetist agreed. 'We need to get her fluids and infection under control.'

From Theatres Josh went directly to his afternoon clinic. 'Seventy today,' the nurse in charge of his clinic said cheerfully. 'It's going to be another long afternoon, Josh. Were you and William held up in Theatres?'

'We had an emergency admission,' he confirmed. He reached for the phone on his desk. 'Let me make one call then we'll get started.' He punched out the numbers to check his home number again, leafing through the case notes for his first patient while he waited for Paige to answer. Only she didn't answer. When he showed his last case out of clinic just after six he tried Paige again but there was still no reply.

He went up to Intensive Care to check that Mrs Lacy was stable, which she was, although the staff had elected to continue ventilating her by machine overnight. Then he called in at the ward because Bunty had bleeped him to let him know that Emma McDermott was ready to go home and that she and her parents wanted to thank him personally before they left.

The police still hadn't found the driver or the van responsible for her injuries, but Emma remained philosophical. 'I had a big essay due last week but they gave me an automatic pass,' she told him brightly. 'I would have failed otherwise.'

'I suppose that's what's called looking on the bright side,' he commented, exchanging a dry look with her exasperated-looking parents. 'All the best, Emma. Have you been given an appointment to see me in clinic?'

'Four weeks,' she confirmed, with a cheerful wave. 'Thanks again for everything, Mr Allard. You've been a real doll. Bye.'

'Bye.' Josh sent Bunty a sideways look as Emma swung away on her crutches. 'What do you think being a doll means?'

'She likes you,' Bunty said smartly. 'And speaking of women liking you, Josh, it's about time you met up again with the bridesmaid I told you—'

'Bunty, you know I'm not interested.' Checking his watch as he strode away, he called back, 'The surgical audit meeting started five minutes ago. I'll be back after it to see the cases from today.'

The audit meeting went over time as usual and he didn't get to the ward to check his patients, including the six new ones his juniors had admitted so far during their day on call, until after eight.

It was almost nine before he reversed into a parking space outside his home. The fact that there was no yellow Mini in sight didn't mean anything because the street was often parked out during the day, meaning Paige might have had to park around the corner. But the outside door was still unlocked and the key was where he'd left it early that morning.

There'd been an accident, he thought immediately, envisaging Paige unconscious and on life support after crashing her car. She'd fallen asleep, he thought sickly. She'd driven into a power pole and was lying critically ill with internal injuries in some hospital somewhere.

Letting himself in quickly, he dropped his briefcase inside the door and did an automatic check, but it was obvious she hadn't been there.

He went towards the telephone, intending to call her Yorkshire number before he started on hospitals, but as he picked it up he heard her calling, a knapsack was thrown in through the doorway and then she was there.

'Paige!' he exclaimed accusingly, throwing down the phone and crossing over to her. 'Where on earth have you been? I've been worried sick!'

Paige looked surprised. 'Have you?' she said faintly. 'Really?'

'You're twelve hours late.'

'*That* late?' She took his arm, lifted it and frowned at his watch before she let him go again. 'I am,' she said. 'Really. Hmm. That's surprising. It feels much more like six, doesn't it?'

'You're mad.'

'The traffic coming on at Birmingham was awful.'

'Paige—'

'Back in a minute,' she said quickly. 'I'm double-parked. I just need to get the rest.'

'I was about to call hospitals,' he said, going after her.

'Oh, did your bleeper thing go?'

'Not *my* hospital.' Exasperated, he took the blankets she was hauling out of the Mini. 'Other hospitals. I was worried you'd been in an accident.'

'But why would I want to be in an accident?'

'You don't *choose* to be in accidents,' he flared, accepting the rest of the blankets. 'If you did they wouldn't be called accidents. They'd be called ''on purposes'' and they wouldn't happen anywhere near as often.'

'Josh!' She tapped his cheek with her palm, her eyes wide and green and startled. 'Josh, calm down. I'm here. I'm perfectly fine. What's wrong? What's happening with you?'

He closed his eyes briefly. 'I don't know,' he admitted finally. He expelled his breath in a long sigh. 'Believe me, I do not know. I've just discharged a young patient who was badly injured in a hit and run recently so perhaps I'm more sensitive than usual about road dangers. The truth is, I've only been home five minutes myself. I'm sorry, Paige. That was…strange.'

'Very strange.' But she smiled. 'I expect you've had a difficult day at work. Is your patient all right now? Can you carry any more or is that your lot?'

'Give me the rest.' He crouched so she could pile on the remainder of the blankets, but halfway back towards the house he stopped, realising what he was carrying. 'And Emma's fine now, yes. Apart from a leg injury. She went home today. Paige, you won't need these. I have duvets.'

'I need my blankets,' she told him firmly, lugging another knapsack after him. 'I feel the cold in bed.'

'Feather and down duvets.'

'I'm sure they're very nice,' she reassured him, 'but I do need my blankets.'

'Whatever makes you happy.' Shaking his head, Josh took the load inside, peering around the side of the stack so he could see where he was going.

When he came downstairs he retrieved two knapsacks from the floor and carried them both up to her room. When he came back again she still wasn't inside, but when he looked outside he could see her jogging towards him from a long way down the street. The security lights above his door must have been illuminating him because she lifted a hand and waved at him.

Shaking his head again, Josh waved back. He waited for her to come to him. 'There was a space here,' he said, indicating the narrow gap between his car and the one ahead. 'Why did you park way down there?'

'The exercise was good,' she said breathlessly. 'After

driving for hours I needed to stretch my legs. Josh, I thought a week would be nice. To think. Is that all right? Are you sure you don't mind? If you think that's too long—'

'A week is fine,' he interrupted. 'A month would be fine. Six months would be fine. Paige, it's up to you. However long you need. You must see how much room there is here.'

'You are kind.' She touched his cheek again, her hand cool against his skin. 'Don't argue,' she chided, when he started to. 'Whatever you say, you're truly kind. I have no idea how I'm going to pay you back for this.'

They went inside and he closed the doors behind them. 'Paying me back's easy,' he said smoothly. 'When you decide you're ready for sex again, you can sleep with me.'

CHAPTER FOUR

PAIGE looked around sharply, a strange look on her face, but then her face cleared as if she'd decided something and she laughed, then said, 'And I really believe you want me, Josh.'

'Paige…?' Josh leaned back against the door and folded his arms, puzzled by her laughter. 'Why wouldn't I?'

'Look at me!' She laughed again. 'I mean, all joking aside, Josh, and it's sweet of you to try to make me feel better by pretending, but just look at me.' She stretched out her arms and twirled around. 'Look at the way I look these days. Have you ever seen anything so revolting?'

'You look wonderful,' he said slowly. Her eyes sparkled, she was laughing and her normally pale cheeks were still pink from her run. The worn jeans she wore clung lovingly to her exquisite legs, and even if her long, woolly jumper concealed her lovely breasts and the curves of her bottom it didn't stop him imagining them. 'Why are you laughing?'

'My hair is disgusting,' she said immediately. 'These clothes are about a hundred years old. I've been awake for twenty-eight hours. My skin is so dry it's practically falling off my face and I haven't shaved my legs in…at least two years. How's that for starters?'

'If you've been awake for twenty-eight hours you probably need sleep,' he said finally, after finding himself briefly lost for words. 'I've put your blankets upstairs.'

She smiled. 'Thank you.'

'Need food?'

'Just sleep.'

He waited until she was a little way up the stairs. 'The suggestion still stands, Paige.'

She laughed again and waved her hands behind her. 'I'll let you know, Josh. In the meantime, if you get a better offer, you'd best take it. Believe me, I'm not worth waiting for. Goodnight.'

She slept for days. He would have been worried except he could tell she must have been getting up to eat from time to time because when he got home from work each evening there were crumbs of toast about, his Marmite kept being left out without its lid and there were new plates in the dishwasher.

On Sunday he rose early and went into the hospital for his usual round. 'Mrs Lacy's been up today to the bathroom,' the nurse in charge of the ward for the weekend told him, referring to his patient who'd had surgery earlier in the week for her bowel obstruction. 'She felt a bit sick last night when we started her on fluids so we went back to just giving her ice to suck.'

Josh nodded. Given how unwell his patient had been pre-operatively, he wasn't surprised her recovery was proving slow. 'There are a couple more bowel sounds this morning,' he told Mrs Lacy once he'd talked to her and examined her abdomen. 'Try taking some water again this morning. If you feel sick again stop, but I suspect you'll be fine this time. This evening, all being well, you'll be able to have a cup of tea, and we'll aim for a light breakfast in the morning.'

'I think I'll be fine this time, Mr Allard.' Mrs Lacy put aside her knitting and wiggled up a little in her bed. 'I am feeling brighter this morning. My neighbour's coming in to set my hair and that always cheers me up.'

'Good.' He smiled. 'That right drain can come out,' he instructed Mrs Lacy's nurse. 'The left one stays for now.

And the catheter can come out as Mrs Lacy's walking now. I'll see you tomorrow, Mrs Lacy.'

She waved. 'Bye, Mr Allard.'

After Josh finished his rounds he spent the remainder of the morning sorting out his most pressing paperwork, then drove home. He sat outside in his garden, enjoying the warm afternoon sunshine on his face as he sipped at a lager and read through that morning's *Independent*.

He didn't hear Paige come out until her soft greeting. When he turned around it was the first time he'd seen her in three and a half days.

'I just spent an hour in one of your wonderful showers,' she said huskily. 'I've probably used every bit of your hot water but I couldn't help myself. It felt wonderful.'

'Good.' He smiled, pleased by how refreshed she sounded. In a white, fluffy bathrobe, with her hair twisted up in a towel on her head and her small feet bare, she looked like a very clean child. 'Are you all right?'

'I'm very well.' She smiled back. 'I didn't realise how tired I was. I haven't been sleeping much for the last year or two, really, but now I feel as if I've caught up. Is there food?'

'I haven't shopped,' he admitted. 'Apart from toast and Marmite, I didn't know what you'd want. Are you still vegetarian?'

'Sort of.' But she looked unsure. 'Not completely. Eggs, cheese and things I still eat. Sometimes even fish.'

'What do you feel like?'

'Scrambled eggs with hot toast and loads of butter.'

'You've eaten me out of toast.' He folded his paper and rose. 'I'll take you shopping.'

Food shopping with a woman could be a seriously intimate exercise, Josh decided later, waiting to one side by the trolley with weary patience while Paige deliberated over her choice of bread. The supermarket wasn't crowded but most people were in couples, and he realised he'd always assumed that men and women buying food together were either married or lovers. What other people thought was irrelevant to him, but still it felt strange to know they'd be making the same sort of assumptions about the two of them.

Also, in the hour they'd already spent moving through the aisles in the random order Paige chose, selecting groceries, he felt he'd come to know her a little better.

'Toast or sandwich?' she demanded finally.

'Toast.'

'Grain or wholemeal?'

'How about soft white?' But her shocked look was enough of an answer. 'Whatever,' he said thinly, prepared to compromise. 'Paige, there aren't any lives depending on this decision. Just as there weren't any depending on what brand of tea you chose.'

'That doesn't mean it's not important to get the choice right.' She stooped now to inspect the lower shelves, but Josh didn't mind that because it gave him a tempting view of her gently curved bottom. 'This one feels nice and it's ten pence cheaper per hundred grams, but it's got salt higher up on its list of ingredients. We don't want too much salt, do we? You're the doctor, Josh. Isn't salt supposed to be bad for blood pressure?'

'Current advice is to cut down on it, yes,' he conceded. 'Which is why we bought the unsalted butter. Paige, just buy the more expensive one.'

'But that one's got amylase in it. What on earth's amylase?'

'It's a digestive enzyme.' That seemed to reassure her, although Josh still had no idea why anyone would want to add a pancreatic enzyme to bread.

He let her worry herself over other ingredients for a few more minutes, before gently taking both loaves out of her hands. He dumped them into the trolley. 'Decide on taste,' he ordered. 'We still have to choose eggs and the store closes in three hours.'

He felt himself pinned by a very green, amused gaze. 'Are you telling me to hurry?'

'We have been in here sixty-five minutes,' he pointed out.

She seemed puzzled by that. 'But don't you find...' she gestured around '...all this variety and food fascinating?'

'No.'

'I could spend hours looking at every little thing.'

'You already have,' he observed. 'I've spent more time in this store today than I've spent in it in six months, and we haven't queued yet.'

'But aren't you having fun?'

His fun had come from watching her expression as she was fascinated by different products and from watching her body as she moved among the shelves, stretching and reaching, but he wasn't about to reveal that. 'The aim of shopping, Paige, is to get in and out as fast as possible, while still buying everything you need.'

She was smiling at him. 'I bet you usually carry a list.'

'Of course I carry a list.' He didn't understand why she seemed to find that funny. 'Normally.' Only because of Paige he hadn't known this time what to put on it. 'How else would I know what to buy?'

'I've never made a shopping list in my life.'

'Why am I not surprised by that?'

Her peal of laughter was uninhibited and infectious, but she seemed oblivious to the startled stares and smiles she was attracting from the other shoppers in the aisle. 'You should see your face,' she told him lightly. 'So disapproving. Josh, you must be bored silly. Go and wait in the car if you like. Listen to the sport on the radio. I can finish here. I don't mind.'

Josh felt his mouth relax into a rueful grin. He felt

abruptly foolish. 'I don't want to go,' he admitted. 'I'm not bored and I suppose I am having fun. Keep going.'

'Eggs.' She nodded at him. 'Two minutes. I promise,' she added, as she dashed off.

Only it took far more than that because when he caught up with her she was trying to persuade two women—both holding boxes of eggs from battery-farmed chickens—that they'd be better off with the free-range ones. 'Twelve to a cage,' she was saying earnestly when Josh stopped his trolley behind her. 'They cut their beaks off to stop them pecking each other. They can't move or walk or do anything but lay eggs.'

The younger of the two promptly exchanged her box for the one Paige was offering her and wheeled her trolley away, but the older woman looked unsure. 'They're an extra pound,' she protested. 'I'm sure you're right about the chickens, dear, but I'm on a pension.'

Josh sighed. 'Paige, don't—'

'It's all right, Josh.' Paige sent him a pleading look, before turning back to her victim. 'Please, take these,' she insisted, offering her coins from her pocket. 'Buy them just this once to try them. If they don't taste good enough to be worth an extra pound next time then…forget you ever met me.'

Josh had assumed that the other woman would be offended by the offer of the money, but he was wrong because she took it happily. 'All right, dear,' she told Paige, taking the egg box she was holding. 'Just for you I'll try them.'

'Thank you.' Paige beamed. 'The chickens of the world thank you. Have a lovely day.'

'Are chickens your only crusade?' Josh asked, as he turned the trolley and followed Paige towards the queue at the closest checkout.

'I saw a documentary about battery farming and it

shocked me silly,' she said seriously. 'Have you ever considered what awful lives those chickens lead?'

Josh refrained from making any comments about the lives many people were forced to lead, or the cruelty some children endured, or the suffering of prisoners of conscience and other such injustices in the world. Such comparisons, he suspected, would merely give someone like Paige cause for more grief, rather than acting as a distraction.

They worked together to load the groceries onto the short conveyer belt at the checkout, and he went through and packed things into bags as the attendant charged them. He had a card ready and when the amount was totalled he went to pass it across, but Paige was faster and she handed cash to the woman. 'Paige—'

'My treat,' she said, sending him a blandly irritating smile when the money disappeared into the cashier's drawer. 'Close your mouth, Josh. Don't be so old-fashioned.'

He frowned. 'You're my guest.'

'So I already owe you.'

'You don't owe anything.'

'But you haven't seen how much I can eat yet,' she countered crisply. She beamed her thanks to the cashier then took two of the bags he'd filled and swung past him. 'I'm starving. I'll have all this gone by Tuesday.'

Acknowledging he'd been outmanoeuvred, Josh followed her out to where he'd parked the car, vowing not to let it happen again. He released the lock on the boot of his car then stopped short when Paige bent over to deposit the groceries into it, his eyes narrowing appreciatively again on her jeans-clad bottom.

Who was he trying to kid? he asked himself, realising the ludicrousness of his vow. His control of the Paige situation was non-existent. He'd let her outmanoeuvre him anywhere, any way, any time she wanted.

Paige decided the scrambled eggs Josh had made for her were the best she'd ever tasted. 'Truly,' she insisted, when he gave her one of those narrowed blue looks he was so good at, meaning she knew he didn't believe her. 'I'm good at scrambling eggs, but these are fantastic,' she added earnestly, wanting to convince him she was serious. 'What's your secret?'

'I expect it's the free-range chickens.'

'I expect it just might be.' His absolute lack of expression made her laugh again. She laughed a lot around Josh, she realised. In the last two and a half years the occasions for laughter in her life had been rare, but in the short time she'd spent with him she seemed to be making up for that.

'You think I'm ridiculous,' she said, understanding what he thought. 'You thought what happened in the supermarket with the eggs was ridiculous. Did I embarrass you?'

'You don't embarrass me.' His look faintly chiding now, he stacked their empty plates and collected their cutlery together. 'You couldn't embarrass me. You're you. How you carry on is nothing to do with me.'

'Thank goodness,' she added mockingly, supplying the words he'd diplomatically left unsaid. 'I noticed today the looks you get from women. I suppose you get chatted up in that supermarket all the time.'

To her surprise he frowned. 'What are you talking about?'

'Women. And you.' She couldn't believe he didn't notice. 'Josh, are you serious? What about that pretty one with the blonde hair? The tall one with all the bananas? She followed you for ages. I kept skipping aisles and doubling back, thinking you might want to be left alone.'

But he still looked blank. 'I didn't see her. Perhaps it was you she was following.'

'Hardly.' Paige nearly choked on the last crumbs of her toast. 'I think I would have noticed,' she said fervently. 'No, her big eyes were definitely trained on you, my darling, gorgeous Josh.'

'Missed my chance,' he said dryly. 'We'll go back tomorrow and you can point her out.'

'You must have been walking around with your eyes closed,' she declared. 'But you'd better watch out. She might have been sexy, but she wasn't a teeny-bopper. You've got to watch out for women at that age. She had a ''ticking biological clock'' look about her.'

She beamed at his startled expression then took the plates he'd collected away from him, shaking her head at him when he rose as if to help. 'I'll do them. Relax. Read your paper. You have to go to work tomorrow so you should be taking it easy.'

'Stacking a dishwasher's not going to exhaust me,' he countered evenly, following her into the kitchen despite her telling him not to. 'Shall I take time off while you're here?'

'Goodness, no.' She looked around, startled. 'Not on my account.'

'I've more than two months' leave due. I imagine Administration would be overjoyed if I said I wanted to take some.'

But, much as she'd like to spend time with him, she couldn't let him waste his holidays on her. 'Josh, I'll be fine on my own. I want to visit lots of galleries and go to Kew, and I'm going to look around shops and get my hair cut and see friends and just…enjoy London. You don't have to entertain me.'

'A week's not long enough for you to fit all of that in.'

'Then I won't do everything.' She smiled. 'It's sweet of you to worry about me, Josh, but you needn't. I've been a bit depressed for a while but I'm starting to feel as if I'm getting my normal self back again. I'm fine.'

'You look better for the sleep.'

'I feel better.' She bent over to put the dishes into his machine. 'Loads better. I'll stick the cutlery in this thing here. What about the pan?'

'Anywhere it fits,' he told her. She felt him moving behind her to pass it to her. 'Paige, you have quite the loveliest bottom I've ever seen.'

Paige came up quickly, pan still in hand. 'Really?' she exclaimed, delighted. With her free hand she lifted her jumper and twisted around, trying to look at her bottom, only she couldn't see past her denim-covered hip. 'Really, Josh, or are you just being kind again?'

'Really.' But instead of looking at her bottom, his speculative gaze had lifted to the pale strip of skin at her waist where she'd lifted her jumper. 'In fact, you're quite exquisite all over.'

She wanted to say something light, to pass off the comment mockingly, only he looked serious, and her mouth dried out and she couldn't talk. She released her jumper, thinking that it would fall to cover her, only Josh caught the edge of it. He didn't lift it higher, simply kept it where she'd held it, but his eyes studied the part of her she'd already revealed.

Her pulse started skipping beats. 'Josh…?'

As if her whisper brought him back to the strange reality of what he was doing, his preoccupied expression cleared. He dropped the edge of her jumper fast. 'A movie, I think,' he said, moving away. 'Sunday evening's always a good time for the cinema. We'll try Mayfair. If our timing's wrong there's a pub close by where we can while away an hour or two.'

'I'd like that.' She studied his face but he was giving

nothing away, so she stooped again, put the pan into the dishwasher and then closed it. 'I'll fetch my coat.'

They arrived an hour before the start of the comedy they'd decided to see, which meant they had time for a leisurely drink in the pub he'd recommended, before returning to the cinema.

'Talk about luxury,' Paige whispered, when they were shown to their seats as the commercials for future attractions were beginning to be shown. She sank into the chair and stretched her legs out in front of her, wiggling her feet, appreciating the soft roominess of the extra-wide seats as she settled in to watch the film. 'Popcorn, please.'

'Popcorn.' He passed her the enormous box she'd insisted they buy. 'Child.'

Afterwards, still laughing from the movie, they returned to the pub for another drink. Paige ordered half a lager mixed with lemonade and lime, and stayed calmly immune to Josh's teasing about what he obviously considered an appalling concoction while he drank his own ale.

He rang an Indian restaurant he knew in Bayswater and on the way home they collected the food. Paige nursed the warm bag of plastic pots and nan on her knees the rest of the way home, and they ate sitting on the floor in his living room, the food spread around them on newspapers.

'That was wonderful.' Finally, when she could manage no more, Paige pushed the remains of her meal away from her and tipped her head back, resting it on the cushions she'd arranged around one of the room's heavily upholstered chairs. 'Thank you, Josh, for a lovely day.'

'Thank *you*, Paige.'

'You're so nice,' she mused. 'Why aren't you seeing anyone?'

'I've told you already.' She looked up in time to catch him smiling. 'I was dumped at the wedding.'

'Well, she was stupid,' Paige declared with a sigh.

Knowing she could hardly lie on his floor for ever, comfortable as it was, she levered herself up into a crouch and gathered the pots and the plates they'd used. 'I'll fix this up then I'm off to bed because I'm very tired. I know that seems strange, considering I slept just about continually for almost four days, but there you go. Life's such a mystery.'

'I might be late tomorrow,' he told her, moving to collect the newspaper she'd left behind. She sensed him following her as she carried everything to the kitchen. 'I'm on call and Mondays are often busy. Leave that, Paige. I'll clean up here. You go to bed.'

Paige wasn't about to argue. Her eyelids were drooping. She went up on her toes and kissed his cheek, supporting herself with an outstretched hand on his broad chest. 'After scoffing all that food I'll probably have nightmares,' she said huskily, stepping back from him before she gave into the temptation to cuddle him properly. 'Don't worry if you hear screams in the night.'

'I'll come and comfort you.'

'That's such a sweet offer.' She waved at him. 'But if I were you I wouldn't. I'm hideously ugly when I first wake. You'd end up screaming as much as me.'

Josh was gone when she came downstairs just before eight the next morning, but he'd left a set of keys on the table, along with a note giving her his contact telephone and bleep numbers at his work should she want to get in touch with him.

It was a sunny, warm day so she went to Kew. She spent several hours wandering around, enjoying the heat of the tropical glasshouses especially, then she caught a train back into town.

She had her hair cut in a salon which had a sign outside saying that no appointments were necessary. Then she strolled along Oxford Street, taking her time, lingering in book shops and department stores and enjoying the liberating sensation of having no chores and no need to rush anywhere.

She hadn't begrudged one moment of looking after her father and she still missed him terribly, but the time with him had been demanding. His neighbours had been happy to sit with him when she'd had to leave the house but, wary of taking advantage of them, she'd always been in a hurry to complete her chores quickly so she could relieve them.

She'd known she'd been putting her own life on hold, yet she hadn't minded that.

But in the months leading up to his death—once it had become obvious that his decline had been inevitable—she'd felt a greyness slowly descend over her usually colourful world. Rather than feeling as if her life had just been on hold, in those bleak months she'd felt as if she hadn't even wanted a life at all outside the narrow world in which she'd been living. She'd not been suicidal—although she knew her GP had been worried about that—she'd merely been uninterested in anything other than her father and her grief.

The greyness had stayed there for the funeral and through the three months following that. The breakthrough had come when she'd received the invitation to David's wedding. That glimpse of her old world had brought with it a little of the colour of her old life. The thought of driving to London for the wedding had seemed impossible at first but gradually it had grown more possible.

Once the improvement had started it had progressed rapidly. In the days before she'd actually set out on the journey she'd felt herself getting better more and more quickly.

And now...? She looked down at the book her hands had picked up automatically. Now, after these days with Josh, she felt ready for living again. So what was she going to do with herself?

'I've been using your computer,' she told Josh two evenings later over dinner. 'I've sent my CV off to a few galleries and museums. I don't think I'll have much luck with them, but I did speak to one of my ex-tutors yesterday at the university and she sounded quite interested. She thinks she might be able to organise part-time research assistant work for me for a few months if I want while I decide what I want to do long term.'

'So you're staying.' He looked pleased. 'Good.'

'There's not much call for an art-history graduate in Malton,' she mused. 'If I stayed there I'd be looking for work in a pub or a shop or perhaps at the bacon factory. Even if I travelled to York each day I'd be unlikely to find anything as interesting as this research work, even if it is only short term.'

'And after that?'

'I'm thinking about doing something completely different. I loved doing my degree but now I think I was a bit silly to do something so…abstract. Art history teaches you about other cultures and civilisations and history, but it doesn't set you up for a lifetime of full employment. At least, an ordinary BA doesn't. If I'd been sensible I'd have done…accountancy. Or something to do with computers.'

'Computers?' He took a sip of the red wine he'd opened to go with the vegetable lasagne she'd made, his brows rising. 'Would that be you, Paige?'

'I don't know.' She lifted one shoulder uncertainly. 'But I have to think practically, and I used to be quite good at using computers. Today I met a friend who did the same degree as me. After graduation she did a course for a year and now she's a computer operator. It pays well and the hours are flexible. She's got a gorgeous little toddler, but she and her husband need the money so she works part time at night.'

'But are you interested in working in an office?'

'Well…' She rolled her eyes a little. The truth was that she had little enthusiasm for the idea. But that didn't make

the prospect any less sensible. 'I could bear it, I suppose.
I can't spend the rest of my life twiddling my thumbs. I
used to be full of lovely ideas about researching great
works of art or acting as a guide for tours of fantastic galleries, inspiring children with a love of art, but obviously I
was a bit naïve in those days.'

'What about marriage and children of your own?'

'Marriage?' It came out as almost a yelp. She blinked
up at him. 'Come on, Josh. Who to? I'm not exactly over-
run with offers.'

'You've been out of circulation.'

'But still.' She rolled her eyes again. 'As distant as the
prospect is at present, I do love the thought of having children. But I can't hang about not doing anything while I
wait for the man of my dreams.'

'You don't consider that raising children would be a full-
time occupation?'

'It might be if and when I have them,' she conceded.
'But that's not about to happen in a hurry.'

'You don't feel your biological clock ticking, then?'

She laughed at that. 'Josh, I'm not even hearing my
alarm clock ticking these days. And I'm hardly in my do-
tage. I've a few years before I have to worry about my
fertility.'

But something in the way he looked away from her and
went straight to his wine again made her hesitate. 'Josh,
what…?' She stroked his hand where it curled around his
wineglass. 'Are you feeling *your* biological clock ticking?'

His smile was gently wry. 'I suppose I am.'

'Oh.' She felt her lips freeze momentarily in an 'O'
shape. So perhaps that woman in the supermarket would
have been perfect for him after all? 'Really?'

'You think it's strange that a man should decide he wants
children?'

'Not at all.' She shook her head firmly. 'There's no reason why men shouldn't feel the same way as women. I'm just, well…'

'Surprised?'

'A little.' She tilted her head, regarding him speculatively. 'But I remember David telling me about your family. You're the oldest of…what? Six?'

'Five.'

'So you're used to a big family. Are you an uncle yet?'

'Nine times over,' he said evenly. 'It's fun but I'd like my own.'

Paige smiled. A man like Josh, so stable and good-humoured and capable, would make a wonderful father. She imagined that his nieces and nephews adored him. 'So?' she said expansively, spreading her hands. 'Any one in mind?'

'For the mother?'

'Of course, for the mother.' At his guarded expression, she laughed. 'Hey, Josh. You do need a woman to produce these children, remember.'

'I haven't,' he said slowly, 'made any selection yet.'

'Well, we'll have to change that.' She brushed her hands together in a demonstration of brisk efficiency. She did feel a faint pang at the thought of Josh being married, but since any imaginings in that direction herself were ludicrous, and since she was far too sane and sensible to let such inane musings distract her from real life and what she could do to help him, she put on a broad smile in reply to his wary look.

'If you're that keen, I'm going to help you,' she declared smartly. 'You've been generous enough to offer me your hospitality. The least I can do is repay you by finding you a wife.'

'Paige—'

'Shut up, Josh. No protests. I want to do this.' She pushed her plate away and stretched as far as she could from the table towards the shelf where the telephone sat, supporting herself with a hand around the table leg when her chair wobbled dangerously as she grabbed the sheaf of notepaper and the pen usually used for taking messages.

'Now,' she said triumphantly, hauling the paper back to the table, 'let me guess. Tall, blonde, gorgeous, utterly glamorous and desperate to breed?'

He sent her a hard look. 'Where do the first four things come from?'

'David,' Paige declared blithely, writing down the description. 'And my personal observations. Josh, you must admit, you do keep to a pattern.'

'You don't know anything about the last few years.'

'I can imagine.' She nodded. 'That girl in the supermarket on Sunday fitted the description absolutely. Right down to the ticking clock. You might just have missed a great chance then. It was probably fated, only I arrived and messed everything up. She might have been your special woman.'

'I'll go back this Sunday,' he said dryly. He reached for her notepad. 'Paige—'

'No, no, don't stop me,' she protested, lifting it away before he could get it. 'Trust me, Josh. I know what I'm doing.'

'"Trust me, Josh."' He rolled his eyes. 'The last time you said that to me you dumped that flea-bitten mongrel Tiger on me. "Trust me, Josh," you said then, too. "He looks so sad. His owner will come looking for him tomorrow. It's just for one night."'

'Tiger!' Paige's eyes widened delightedly. 'I can't believe I forgot about Tiger.' She'd found the puppy crying in the park where she used to go on sunny mornings to study. He'd been thin and sad and neglected, and when David had refused to have him anywhere near their flat she'd had to ask Josh to look after him. She'd put up signs around the area and in the local pet shop and vet practice, but no one had come to claim him. 'Where is he now? How is he? Does he still dribble everywhere?'

'Still with my parents. Fine. No, my parents had his teeth seen to.'

'He was so cute.'

'He wasn't cute.' Josh looked perplexed by the description. 'He was malnourished and neglected and he had a severe flea infestation problem. I had to get pest exterminators in here to see to the carpets after I took him home.'

'Would your parents mind me driving down to see him?'

'They wouldn't mind at all. They and I might think you're mad to go all that way to visit a mongrel like Tiger, but they wouldn't mind.'

'You're horrible.' But she laughed. 'Do they love him?'

'For reasons that escape me completely, they do seem to, yes,' he said heavily. 'Or at least they haven't had him put down yet.'

'You pretend to be so awful, but inside you've got a good heart,' she told him. 'You could have refused to take him, like David did, but you didn't. You could have sent him off to be impounded, but you didn't. You looked after him.'

'Because you, Paige, looked up at me with those big green eyes and you begged me,' he told her. Because you said, ''Trust me,'' in that soft little voice of yours. How could I possibly have refused you anything?'

She smiled across at him, knowing that he was merely teasing her. 'David did.'

'David's made of sterner stuff than me.'

'Only when it came to Tiger.' She laughed. 'About everything else, David's a cotton-wool ball compared with you. Now, stop trying to distract me. Where were we with this?' She lowered her eyes to the list she'd started to prepare. 'So far we've got tall, blonde, gorgeous, glamorous and wants children. What else do you want? What about brains? Are they important? What about size of boobs? Does that matter?'

He sent her a weary look. 'Tea?'

'Please.' She smiled, watching him as he levered himself away from the table and moved easily towards the kitchen. 'Come on, Josh. Play. This is fun.'

'I can see you're enjoying yourself,' he observed, putting water on to boil.

'I am a little,' she conceded, a little surprised by the realisation that it was true. 'You're fantastically appealing, you know, Josh. I mean, you look great, you're nice, you're a doctor and you've got all this money...' She laughed at his hard look. 'Be reasonable. You could have any woman you wanted. I'm just trying to narrow the field a little to make my job easier.'

'I don't need your help.'

'But I want to give it.' She tried for a note of authority in her voice. 'I know I can help.' She went back to her note. 'So, for intelligence, what should I put? Yes? No? Or indifferent?' When he didn't answer she smiled. 'I'll put yes,' she decided. 'You don't want a nincompoop. Boobs?'

'Yes.'

'Yes, what?' She lifted her brows. 'Yes, big? Yes, small? Yes, silicone? Yes, what?'

'Yes, present.'

'I'll put indifferent.' She wrote that. 'That's good. That makes it easier. Hobbies?'

'Shall we have this in the other room?' He'd added boiling water to the teapot and now he poured her tea immediately and passed it towards her. She saw that it was exactly the faintly coloured sort of brew she preferred.

'Good idea.' She put the pen between her teeth and the notepad under her arm, and carried her tea towards the more formal living room. 'We might catch the news on TV.'

But the evening had gone more quickly than she'd realised because the broadcast was already over. She channel-flicked backwards and forwards, using the remote, smiling at Josh when she saw the irritated look her changing channels provoked. 'What?'

'Must you do that?'

'Yes.' She took the pen out of her mouth and poked her tongue out at him in retaliation for his sudden pompousness. 'I must.'

Just to annoy him, she flicked through every channel again, but he moved too fast for her and his cool fingers circled her wrist. He removed the device firmly from her hand and took it away. 'That's not fair,' she protested, laughing. 'There were commercials on that channel before. I couldn't tell what the programme was.'

'It's all rubbish.' He clicked the set off completely, left the remote beside it, then came around and took the seat beside her on the couch. 'If you do decide to stay here, Paige, what are you going to do with your parents' house?'

'I'll have to go up and sort things out then I'll see if I can find an agent to lease it out,' she said airily. 'OK, Josh. No more changing the subject.' She retrieved her notepad from the floor where it had dropped in their brief struggle over the remote, then tucked her legs up beside her and leaned back into her corner, watching him. 'You didn't answer my question about hobbies.'

He looked amused. 'Where are you going to find this woman?'

'I have contacts.' She closed her eyes, thinking. 'Lots of friends from my student days who must have friends as well. Failing that, I could go to an agency for you.'

'A dating agency?'

'Mmm.' She wrinkled her nose at his disgusted expression. 'There are good, professionally run agencies especially set up to handle just your sort of requirement. Agencies don't cater just for desperate, unlovable people, Josh. Loads of people these days are too busy with their careers to have time to look for partners.' She raised her hand firmly when he opened his mouth. 'Don't argue. There's no obligation on you. I'll handle all the details and you'll just have to choose from my final selection.'

'Paige—'

'It's entirely my pleasure,' she said quickly. 'Think of it as me repaying you for letting me stay here.'

'In that case, you can leave tomorrow.'

'Nasty man.' But she laughed. 'You wouldn't throw me out onto the street. Be serious. Just once. Tell me what you want.'

'What I want...'

'What you want, in a woman, at this stage in your life,' she said firmly. 'Or more, at this moment, what is your fantasy woman like?'

'At this moment?'

'Mmm.'

'At this very moment.' She was pleased to see he seemed prepared to give that serious consideration. He'd put his tea on the coffee-table beside him and now he rested back against the couch, his legs crossed lazily at the ankles and stretched in front of him, his eyes closing. 'What I want,' he repeated. 'I wonder, Paige, if you're quite ready to know that.'

CHAPTER FIVE

'OH, I'M ready,' Paige assured Josh, her pen poised. 'Truly,' she added, when he still didn't say anything.

He didn't open his eyes but eventually he said slowly, 'For starters, she's not tall or blonde or any of those other things you described. Except for the gorgeous bit.'

'She would have to be gorgeous,' Paige murmured, writing that down quickly, 'for you. I knew that.'

'She's five feet five or thereabouts, she has skin like cream, a little button nose, green eyes a man could drown in, a mouth just begging to be kissed and soft dark hair all around her face which is rumpled a little so that it always looks as if a man's been mussing it. I do like your new hairstyle, by the way, Paige. Did I tell you that?'

'No.' Paige rolled her eyes, realising she'd been had. 'Josh, you're flirting again.'

He opened his eyes, his gaze very blue and very serious. 'I'm not flirting, Paige.'

'Teasing, then.' She lowered her eyes firmly to the list she'd ludicrously started to fill in until she'd realised what he'd been saying. 'And you're not being fair. I've already told you I couldn't possibly resist you. Be serious. Start again. She's gorgeous—'

'And irritating. And annoying. And profoundly stupid.' Before she knew what was happening he'd moved, moved them both, lifting her and straightening her legs so she lay on her back on the couch, blinking up at him in bewilderment.

'You've been particularly dense about me, Paige.' He was supporting his weight on his elbows so that although

73

he lay above her, surrounding her, he wasn't actually atop her. 'That's probably my fault for trying too hard to keep my hands off you.'

'You mean you really do want me?' she squeaked, her head spinning now. 'You, Josh? You mean…physically? You mean you actually do rather fancy me? *Me?*'

'Mmm.' His mouth was so close to hers she felt his murmur against her lips. 'I think you're enchanting.'

She tilted her face up a little, closing her eyes in thoughtful excitement as he pressed tiny kisses to the sensitive skin all around her mouth, wondering, despite her doubts, whether there was anything in the world that would ever feel quite so heart-stoppingly wonderful as Josh kissing her. 'That was…pretty good,' she whispered brokenly, meeting his watchful look half shyly when he lifted his head. She wondered if, after all, perhaps she was more ready for *shenanigans* than she'd thought. She decided that perhaps, just perhaps, she might even be completely ready. 'I think I can handle a little more, please.'

'Like this?' He touched his mouth to her throat, then moved to her chin, then her nose. 'Or this?'

'Four out of ten,' she complained, catching at his face with her hands to hold him still, frustrated by his teasing avoidance of her mouth. 'Must try harder.'

'"Must try harder"?' He drew back sharply, his expression offended as he surveyed her laughing face. 'I think you're forgetting who's in charge here.'

'No tickling,' she shrieked, alarmed when he lunged towards her. She rolled from side to side, trying to escape the couch as he grabbed her. 'No tickling. Please, no tickling. Josh, no!'

'You deserve it.' He was remorseless. '"Must try harder"!' he repeated, his tone disgusted as she dissolved into giggles. There was no escape. He was far too big and strong for her to fight. When he'd finished with her ribs, he got hold of her feet, holding her legs so she couldn't kick him. He swiftly dispensed with the thick socks she'd been wearing to keep her feet warm, and tickled her mercilessly until she was weak and feeble and breathless and drained of all fight on the floor alongside him.

'It's not fair,' she protested faintly, smiling into his triumphant eyes where he lay beside her on his side, propped on one, lazy elbow, watching her, their legs still entwined. 'I shouldn't lose. I was only trying to get you a bit more passionate.'

'I was already passionate.' He touched her mouth with his thumb. 'I was trying to control myself. You are incredibly sexy, Paige Connolly.' His other hand uncurled and he used both to take her hips and lift her against him. 'Just—'

'Just don't take you too seriously,' she supplied with careful cheerfulness, knowing exactly what he wanted to warn her about. 'All you want is a few hours of passionate sex. But I'm not to take you seriously because I'm too unbearable to ever be your chosen wife or the mother of your wonderful children.'

'Unbearable's a good word,' he agreed dryly. 'Unbearably beautiful breasts.' His hand had come back to her mouth but now it strayed slowly from her mouth down to the crew neck of her jumper then lower to lightly brush the mounds he was contemplating. 'Unbearably delicious bottom. Unbearably sexy thighs.'

'Personally, I'm beginning to like the sound of the passionate bit,' she said huskily, her breath coming faster again. 'Josh…?'

'Mmm?' He was softly cupping her, his thumb nudging the tiny erect buds of her breast through the wool of her jumper, while Paige busied herself with the buttons fastening his plaid shirt.

'You know how I said the other day that I wasn't ready for sex yet?'

He nuzzled her neck. 'Mmm.'

'Well, in a little while I think I might be ready to start thinking about it again,' she said breathlessly.

'In a little *while*?' Josh made a sound like a groan. 'What's wrong with now? Paige, you're driving me mad.'

'You're a terrible exaggerator,' she whispered, coming over to straddle his hips, flushing slightly at the startling and insistent pressure of his arousal between her thighs. 'I'm sure I'm not about to drive anyone mad. But I want to look at you now,' she added unevenly, her hands stilling on his shirt. 'Is that all right?'

'Of course it's all right.' He seemed bemused by the question.

'I want to take this off.' She rose slightly, concentrating on the final buttons holding his shirt together. 'No, not me,' she protested, slapping his hands away when they slid behind her to cup her bottom. 'Behave.' Her breath caught in her throat as she revealed the broad smoothness of his chest. Slowly, very slowly, she pulled the edges of the shirt apart and pushed the fabric to his shoulders, leaning over him, letting her hair tease his face as she eased the plaid away. 'I want to see you without this.'

'You're so bossy,' he complained, but the word was warm and husky against her ear and it made her laugh.

'And you're so beautiful.' She settled back on his hips, deliberately taking her time, making whirls with her hands against the firm, muscled power of his chest, noting, with curious delight, the immediate flat hardening of his nipples.

'Look, you've done the same to mine,' she exclaimed, lifting her jumper so he could see the prickling she could feel. Bare beneath the wool, her breasts had grown heated and swollen, her nipples peaked.

'Then let me kiss you.' Josh's hands, abruptly urgent, curled around her upper arms and pulled her down onto him properly while he lifted her forward so her breasts came to his mouth.

She hung there, her head spinning, not able to see him because her jumper had fallen to cover his face, her breath coming in soft, shallow gasps at the faint, unfamiliar squeezing sensation pulling deep in her abdomen and between her thighs as he suckled her. 'Josh...?'

'Mmm?' His voice was muffled against her.

'I think that little while I was talking about might just have passed now.'

The mouth at her breast stilled. Slowly he came out from beneath her jumper. She saw that his face was tinged with colour, but instead of the warmly teasing expression it had worn before it had gone abruptly guarded.

'I think I'm ready for this now,' she affirmed breathlessly. 'Everything. Please. Now.'

'Paige—'

'I'm very sure.' She pulled her jumper over her head herself, baring her upper body completely. 'I hope I won't be too boring for you,' she whispered. 'I'm a bit out of practice.'

'And crazy.' His hands went around the back of her neck and he lifted himself up from the hips so they sat close together, her legs either side of him. 'Definitely crazy. Trust me, Paige, you will never be boring.'

His eyes laughed at her but his mouth came to hers and there was nothing laughing about him then, only a long, soft, slow exploration which left her dizzy and longing for him. He lifted her and carried her upstairs.

In the morning she fell asleep almost as soon as he left her, dimly aware that he had to go to work but beyond processing the information. When she finally woke properly, a squint at the clock beside his bed told her it was almost four in the afternoon.

Not believing that, she sat up abruptly to get closer to the clock, but then she caught her breath and winced, reminded abruptly of the unaccustomed exercise of the night before as her body protested with stiffness.

The clock was right, she saw, remembering then that she hadn't slept until the morning. Flustered at that, as much as at the memory of her own wanton behaviour the night before, she rolled herself gingerly off the bed and hobbled towards the bathroom.

She ran a deep bath and climbed in carefully. She washed her hair then soaped her body gently and rested back against the porcelain and closed her eyes, enjoying the feeling of the warm water soaking some of the strain out of her sore muscles.

After an hour she managed to drag herself out of the comforting embrace of the bath, but she still felt too tired to go as far as to dress. Checking the clock again vaguely to make sure she had time for a quick nap before Josh came home and teased her for spending the whole day in bed, she slid back beneath the sheets of his bed and closed her eyes.

The brush of something against her cheek woke her gently. She opened her eyes and saw Josh and the finger with which he'd stroked her awake, and smiled. 'You're home already?' she asked huskily, coming up on her elbows. 'I only just went to sleep again. I didn't hear you come in.'

Still in the dark suit she guessed he'd worn for work, he was sitting on the edge of the bed, looking amused. 'Good day?'

'A sleepy day,' she confessed. 'I only got up for a bath.' She stretched, then winced. 'I'm still as stiff as anything. I can hardly move. You wore me out, Josh.'

'I wore myself out.' He swivelled and came down over her, his elbows on either side of her arms as he nuzzled her forehead and hair. 'Concentrating today wasn't easy. Mmm. You smell nice. Perfume.'

'Your shampoo and your soap,' she countered breathlessly, lifting her fingers to his tie. 'Are you coming to bed?'

'Didn't you say you couldn't move?'

'All the more reason to stay here,' she whispered, on fire for him again. 'If we do it slowly and very gently it won't hurt. Besides, I couldn't possibly make it downstairs.'

'What about food?'

'Call for pizza,' she told him, her mouth seeking his. 'In a little while.'

They had pizza later. He'd ordered far too much, but Paige was starving and she managed to make a pig of herself by eating it anyway. She spent the next hour while it went down rolling about, clutching her stomach and complaining about how much food he'd bought. By the time she was ready for sex again Josh was stretched out on his back, one arm flung towards her, deeply asleep.

Far too awake herself to contemplate sleeping again, and not wanting to disturb him when he had to work the next morning, she lay beside him for a little while, quietly watching him sleep, then covered him gently with one of the duvets he seemed to be so proud of and left him.

Paige spent the next morning on the telephone, trying to arrange work and somewhere to live in the future, then she treated herself to an afternoon at a visiting exhibition at the National Gallery.

She hadn't seen Josh since leaving him the night before, so she wasn't sure whether he would be home for dinner. He'd told her that when he was on call or needed to work late he often ate at the hospital, only he hadn't told her what nights that would be. She picked up supplies from a supermarket in Covent Garden anyway, in case he made it back to the house.

'You're going to miss vegetarian kofta with basmati rice,' she told him cheerfully, when he telephoned later and said he was on call and he wouldn't be home. 'It's one of those ones you heat in the microwave. It looks yummy. I might eat yours, too.'

'Don't you dare.' But he sounded amused. 'Bring it to me.'

Paige blinked. 'To the hospital?'

'Why not?'

'I suppose there's no reason,' she conceded. Besides, she had to admit to a little curiosity about seeing where he worked.

'We're about to start a laparotomy,' he told her, and she nodded automatically, although she had no idea what the word meant, 'but I should be finished here in Theatre in about an hour. Give me a bit longer before you come in case we find something unexpected.' He gave her directions about where to park and explained where she should go to have him bleeped. 'If there's an emergency in the meantime and I'm still tied up operating, whoever answers my bleeper should be able to tell you how long I'll be.'

But when she got there and had Josh paged, he answered the call himself. 'It was getting so late I thought you'd changed your mind,' he told her lightly. 'I'm starving. Where've you been?'

'Just…getting here,' she said vaguely, guessing from his words that she was running later than she'd thought. 'How was your…laparology?'

'Laparotomy,' he said quietly. 'It means an operation where you open the abdomen. It was fine. Very quick. Where are you?'

'Down where you told me,' she said, looking around the modern foyer. 'By the desk. They called you for me.'

'Stay there. I'll come and get you.'

She was expecting him to look very important and responsible in a white coat with a stethoscope around his neck and a bleeper blaring off urgent messages continually, like a surgeon out of a television drama. Instead, when he appeared he was his usual calm, unflustered, wonderful self.

He'd taken off his jacket so he was in shirtsleeves but there was no coat and no stethoscope and the only clue to his identity was a silent, dark-coloured bleeper clipped discreetly to his belt.

'I thought there'd be drama,' she told him, following him up flights of stairs to his office, which appeared to be somewhere high inside the main building. 'I thought there'd be sirens and emergency calls, and I was expecting you to be running about like a lunatic.'

'My registrar does all that,' he explained. 'With the help of my house officer. Sorry to disappoint you, but I only step in if the juniors need help.'

'But tonight you've been working.'

'In Theatre,' he explained. 'Consultant surgeons do a lot of emergency operating, even if we don't chase around the hospitals much any more. This case tonight could have been tricky so I wanted to be here for it, but the only reason I'm still here now is that I'm expecting a transfer from a consultant at another hospital. He could arrive any time tonight and I want to assess him personally and talk to the surgeon who referred him before I come home.'

'So you're not about to rip anyone's chest open and do open heart massage on the floor here, then?'

'I hope not.' He grinned at her. 'At least, not before we've eaten.'

He took her to a kitchen on a ward, where he used the microwave to heat the food. Then they collected forks and mugs of tea and carried the meals to his office. He dumped a load of files onto the floor to clear her a seat and shifted his computer to make room for her food. She'd bought two separate servings of the meal so they had their own dishes.

'It's good.'

'Mmm,' she agreed, taking another forkful of the hot food herself. 'You should buy meals like this to have when you're working. What would you normally eat here?'

'Whatever's going.' He shrugged. 'Something from a machine if there's nothing else.'

'You said your case tonight could have been tricky. Was it very difficult?'

'It turned out not to be.'

'What was it?'

'A leaking stomach ulcer.' He took a mouthful of his curry, swallowed it, then leaned back in his chair, his eyes narrowing when she sat waiting expectantly for him to continue. 'Are you really interested?'

'Yes.' She smiled. 'Go on. That sounds like a very complicated condition. Why wouldn't the operation be difficult?'

'Because we're running a trial on a simple treatment,' he explained slowly, as if he still wasn't convinced of the depth of her interest. 'In recent years we've discovered that the majority of stomach ulcers are caused by an infection. What we're doing at the moment is randomly allocating patients who come in with leaking ulcers—if they agree—to receive either the traditional operation, which is fairly complicated and aimed at reducing the amount of acid secreted by the remaining stomach, or, alternatively, a simple op where we just put a patch over the ulcer to stop it leaking then give antibiotics and an ulcer-healing drug by mouth. The man tonight agreed to the trial and he ended up being allocated to have the simple operation.'

'Will he be all right?'

'He'll be fine.'

'So you think that's the better treatment?'

'Hopefully, the trial, and others like it going on around

the world, will tell us for sure,' he told her. 'At the moment it's not completely clear.'

Paige frowned, considering that. 'But if stomach ulcers are caused by an infection then it makes sense to treat them with antibiotics rather than big operations, doesn't it? Isn't that obvious?'

'It's not so obvious with ulcers that have burst through and are leaking,' he said mildly. 'Time and studies like this will tell, but at present there's a suspicion that bacteria aren't always present in ulcers that leak. It may be that we're dealing with a different type of ulcer.'

Paige paused in her eating. 'It's interesting, isn't it?'

'Well, I think so.' He looked amused. 'I'm surprised you do.'

'I think your job sounds fascinating.' She took some more food and a little while later asked, 'Can you actually rip someone's chest open and massage his heart, or is that just a myth? Would they die anyway?'

'He or she would if you did it,' he told her, looking amused again. 'But in the right circumstances, with the right instruments and in the right place, doing just that can save a life. Why?'

'Just curious.' She tilted her head. She'd never thought about his and David's work before, at least not in such graphic terms. 'Have you ever done it? Have you ever just…wrenched one open?'

'Not *wrenched* exactly,' he said dryly. 'Out of surgery once I had to on a patient in a cardiothoracic ICU when I was the registrar. Post-surgery he had a heavy bleed and his heart stopped. We tore out his wires and opened his chest on the unit, yes.'

'Did he live?'

'He's still alive six years later.'

'Incredible.' She stared at him, at his hands as he took another forkful of curry, deeply impressed. 'It must feel amazing to have such power over life and death. Do you get nervous when you're operating?'

'I did occasionally when I was less experienced.' He lifted one shoulder. 'It's years since I've felt any nervousness. And it doesn't feel amazing. Just normal. It's my job. The real test, the difficult part of my work, is deciding what to do and when to stop. Once a surgeon cuts, the stress is largely gone because the operating itself is purely technical.'

'But you're not a plumber,' she protested. 'The things you do affect a real person. Doesn't that worry you?'

She thought that if she were a doctor, that would be her biggest problem, but Josh shook his head. 'When I'm operating I'm concentrating on the technicalities. I enjoy that aspect of the job. The doctor-patient interaction is enjoyable, too, but that comes before and after surgery. In Theatre you focus on the task in hand.'

Paige was fascinated by this glimpse of his professional persona. 'I don't think I could switch off like that,' she confessed huskily. 'I think I'd be too worried about the person to be able to concentrate on the technicalities.'

'Most of us start off like that as students, but the fascination for surgery takes over. Either that or you go into some other area of medicine.'

'David hated surgery,' she recalled. 'He couldn't understand why you were so keen on it. He said he could never work out what was going on and he used to faint. He said he was always going to go into general practice.'

'David's a good GP,' Josh answered. 'One of the best. But he did used to faint in surgery and I spent a lot of time covering for him.' He grinned. 'I always knew he was going to get wobbly when the blood started flying around.'

'Well, I can understand that,' Paige declared heartily with a grimace, grateful that he'd waited for her to finish eating before making that sort of remark. 'What should I do with this?' she asked, meaning her plastic dish.

'Pass it here.' Lifting himself easily out of his chair, he collected the rubbish in a plastic bag and threw it into the bin. They washed their hands in the little basin in the corner, and as Paige dried hers his hands came gently down onto her shoulders.

'Do I get a kiss now?'

'Now that your most urgent desire's taken care of?' she teased, turning around slowly to meet his embrace.

'You're my most urgent desire,' he murmured when he lifted his head after a long, hungry kiss. 'Where'd you go last night? I woke up and you were gone.'

'I didn't want to disturb you.' She kissed him again. 'You were sleeping so peacefully.'

'I like being disturbed by you.'

'Not when you haven't slept in two days.'

'Don't pretend you left for my sake,' he said. 'You wanted your blankets.'

Paige laughed. 'I wanted my blankets,' she admitted. 'I know you think your duvets are wonderful but I still miss my blankets.'

'So put them on my bed.'

'You'll overheat.'

'I'm overheating already.' He took away her coat then sat down again and pulled her down onto his lap, his arms strong and insistent around her back, urging her against him while he kissed her thoroughly.

'Mmm. Nice,' she murmured, licking her lower lip when the kiss ended. 'More.'

'First get rid of some clothes,' he said huskily, his hands going to the buttons of her shirt. 'Aren't you hot? Hmm?'

'A little,' she admitted breathlessly, looking down at the pallor of her lifting breasts as he swiftly bared her. 'Aren't you supposed to be working?'

'They'll bleep me when they need me.' He parted her
shirt and pushed it away from her breasts then bent his head
and touched his tongue to the crest of one tightened mound,
making her squirm. 'Better than vegetarian kofta,' he muttered, lifting her against him, his hands now intent on the
fastening of her jeans. 'Much, much better. Now these.'

'Josh...?' Paige whispered, bringing her hands down to
stop his, wishing, belatedly, that she'd worn a bra because
at least that delay might have given her some chance of
resisting him. Instead, now, with the delicate movements
of his mouth at her breast, she was almost too aroused to
care any more. Mustering some last vestige of sanity, she
twisted to the door behind her, confirming what she'd already known. 'There's no lock. Someone might come in—'

'I'll send them away again.' But he must have realised
her concern was genuine because with a quick smile he
lifted her up and onto his desk, then carried the chair she'd
sat on to eat to the door and wedged it under the handle
so it couldn't be opened. 'Better?'

'Much.' Returning his smile, she shrugged off her shirt
and lay back on his desk, displaying herself, her arms
folded behind her head. 'Now you.'

'But you're not finished.' He took off her shoes then bent
over her and firmly unbuttoned her jeans. 'I want you bare,
Paige.' While she lay silent and dry-mouthed, he lowered
her zip then tugged the jeans away so she wore only her
white lacy knickers, which he proceeded to dispense with
equally efficiently. 'Completely bare.'

'You're on duty,' she reminded him faintly. 'Are you
sure you're allowed to be doing this?'

'Relax.' His expression seriously intent, he put his arms
around her thighs and brought her across his desk towards
where he now sat, holding her thighs apart when in one,
fleeting moment of crimson embarrassment she tried to
close them on him. 'Shush,' he chided softly against her

stomach when she started almost half-heartedly to protest. 'Lie back. Let me.'

Later, when she was still trembling with the pleasure he'd given her, he lifted her into his arms and kissed her tenderly. He held her nestled against his chest until her breathing calmed and she knew something outside of herself again.

'Josh.' She raised her head slowly from the warmth of his shirt. 'I'm sorry. That was all for me—'

'Later.' His mouth was soothing against her forehead. 'And it wasn't all for you but I can't do anything else now. Not here. Not when I might be called soon.'

'Well, any time you want your dinner brought in,' she said weakly, 'make sure you call me. I'll bring it any time night or day. Guaranteed delivery.'

'I might hold you to that.' He kissed her mouth softly. 'Do you do take-away?'

'Whatever you want.'

'Home delivery?'

'Mmm.'

'Then I expect I'll be needing to use your services frequently.' He kissed her again, a gentle, lingering kiss. 'How about we go away in the morning?'

'Away?' She blinked at him.

'I have to do a round at eight but I should be home before ten and then we could leave town. I know a little luxury hotel we could go to till Monday. Or, if you like, we could come back on Sunday and stop off at my parents' for you to see Tiger.'

'I'd love that...' But then she stopped. 'Josh, remember the woman from the supermarket last week? You're going to go back on Sunday to see if you can find her.'

'I don't want her,' he said evenly. 'I want you.'

Her heart melted. 'That's so sweet.' But then she stopped again. 'Josh, please, don't be too lovely,' she pleaded faintly, realising what he was doing to her. 'Not *too* wonderful, not all the time.'

'Paige...?'

'You see, it would be awful if I fell in love with you,' she said helplessly. 'That would be very easy but it would put me in a hopeless position. I'm still getting over losing Mum and Dad. Imagine if you make me fall in love with you and then Ms Perfect walks into your life and I lose you. I might go *completely* barmy.'

'That's not going to happen.' He narrowed his eyes at her. 'Paige, I'm not about to walk away from you.'

'But you will,' she insisted. 'And you must. I've gone into this with my eyes wide open, Josh. You want children urgently. All you need is the right woman. If she walks in here this minute you would be an idiot not to chase her.'

'I'm not in such a hurry.'

'I don't believe you.' She stroked his cheek. 'I saw you looking at all those families in the supermarket on Sunday. At the time I didn't understand why, but I know now. You want that. Kids, potty training, strollers, the works. You want it all.'

'I told you, all I want is you.'

'Temporarily,' she agreed, kissing him. 'We both know I'd drive you mad in the longer term.'

'You're not so bad.'

'I'm not so bad unless I'm running one minute late, in which case you're tearing your hair out,' she reminded him teasingly. 'I'm not so bad unless I spend one minute too long in the supermarket, in which case you're climbing the walls. I'm not so bad unless the washing machine overflows. I'm not so bad unless one day I leave three little toast crumbs in your perfect kitchen—'

'You're always hours, *days*, late, not minutes,' he chided. 'And the washing machine flooded because you dammed the drainage with clothes. And toast crumbs from one end of the place to the other and Marmite jar lids lost for ever, not just a few crumbs in the kitchen. And, Ms Connolly, *an hour and a half* in the supermarket, not one minute.'

'You're worse than David,' she told him, laughing. 'Face it, Josh. You just hide it better. Underneath that smiling, pleasant exterior, you're an order freak. I'd drive you insane.'

'I'd control that.'

'But I might not be able to. I know what it's like to try and share a life with someone who's incompatible. David and I lasted three weeks.'

'You stayed two years.'

'Only as a flatmate,' she protested. 'The romance was gone after the first three weeks. Romance doesn't survive incompatibility. Just like…what we have wouldn't.'

'We're managing now.'

'It's week two.'

'Week two's been pretty good.'

'Because you know it's only temporary.'

'If it's so temporary, what does that make you?'

'Your floozy.' She laughed at his startled expression, half-amazed by her own light-heartedness in the face of what would probably turn out to be a painful ending for her, even if she did manage to avoid falling completely for him. 'The last, passionate fling of your bachelor days,' she cried. 'Your final, wanton—'

But he stopped her with his mouth. 'I get the message,' he said dryly, when he lifted his head from what had been a very drugging kiss. 'You fancy yourself in the role of sex object, do you, Paige?'

'I love it,' she declared languidly, surprised to find that was true. 'No one's ever thought me sexy before.' She leaned back in his arms, spreading hers to display herself to him. 'But look at me. No clothes on and I don't care a bit. I'm shameless.'

'Shamelessly irresistible,' he murmured, studying her breasts. 'I've changed my mind about not making love to you. Let's make the time.'

But the jerk of the door behind the chair brought them sharply apart before he got very far. 'Josh?' a woman's voice called. 'Josh? I can't get in. Your door's jammed.'

Paige went to go for her clothes, but Josh held her still, shaking his head, seeming amused by her urgent determination to get away.

'What do you want, Bunty?' he called calmly, as if he were simply sitting at his desk studying, rather than caressing Paige's naked breasts.

'Your new patient's arrived. He looks all right but I know you wanted to be called. I thought I'd come and get you, rather than bleeping you.' The voice was muffled—suggesting that the door was thick and the chair's control of the opening secure—but still quite audible. 'And Mr Wilkins has spiked another temperature. Your registrar thinks it's just collapse in his lungs, but since you're here I know he wants to get your advice on him before he orders more physio. Are you stuck in there? Can you come out? Shall I call someone out from Maintenance?'

Josh lifted his head from Paige who'd frozen with embarrassment. 'I'll see you on the ward in a few minutes,' he said unhurriedly. 'Go away, Bunty.'

'Yes, Josh.' The voice sounded unsure but after a little while Paige heard steps going away.

Josh smiled at her panicked expression. 'Sorry,' he said briskly, allowing her to go free. 'Bunty's the charge nurse on my ward. She must be working a late. I'd better sort things out here. Will you wait or would you rather meet me at home?'

'Meet you at home,' Paige said shakily as she scrambled into her clothes. 'Thank goodness you jammed the door.'

'Bunty's worked here for twenty years,' he told her

lightly. His hand curled around the back of her neck and drew her forward into a brief kiss. 'She's seen it all. She wouldn't have been too shocked. Remember the way out?'

'I'll find it,' she assured him. 'Go. Quickly.' She shooed him off, worried about delaying his work. 'Hurry. Go to work.'

He laughed. 'Slave-driver. Bye.'

'Bye.' Paige buttoned her blouse, fastened her jeans, smoothed her hair, collected the plastic supermarket bag she'd used to bring her jumper and purse and keys and headed for the door.

But in the corridor she hesitated, looking about doubtfully, unsure which way they'd come. She went a little way to the right, then stopped, turning around to look back the way she'd come.

A nurse, heading towards her, waved at her to stop. 'Are you lost?'

'A bit,' Paige conceded. 'Is it that way out?'

'Back this way then down in the lift,' the woman said cheerfully. 'I'm Bunty,' she added. 'From Josh's ward. Were you visiting him just now?'

'Yes, that's me.' Paige assumed he'd sent Bunty to make sure she got out all right. 'I'm Paige.'

'I didn't mean to interrupt before.'

'Oh, that's all right.' Paige didn't know where to look. Being brazen with Josh was very easy, but she found the talent had evaporated when faced with someone else. 'We were…having dinner. I brought dinner in for Josh. Vegetarian kofta and basmati rice. From the supermarket. As he was on call. I'm sure he doesn't eat very well when he's working.'

Bunty was nodding along to all of this. 'You were at David Leigh's wedding,' she said confidently when Paige had finished. 'One of my nurses described you. You've got a yellow Mini. You drove up to the hotel and you took Josh away with you.'

'I suppose I did,' Paige said faintly. She guessed that was how it might have looked to an observer, even if the truth of the matter was that he'd rather bossily taken over and driven her away with him. 'More or less.'

'I know Josh very well,' Bunty said brightly, 'but he's never mentioned you before. Are you two—?'

'Friends?' Paige interrupted hastily, before Bunty could voice any more embarrassing suggestion. 'Yes, we are. I've known Josh for years. For a short time years ago I used to go out with David.'

'Well, now, isn't that lovely?' Bunty beamed. 'I've known Josh and David since they were fourth-year medical students. Come and have a cup of tea, Paige.' The nurse took her for a cup of tea before Paige could think of anything to say. 'I'm on my break,' Bunty told her. 'I've got some lovely chocolate digestives we can eat. Do you like chocolate biscuits, Paige?'

CHAPTER SIX

JOSH'S new admission was a thirty-six-year-old man who'd recently had a severe episode of inflammation of his pancreatic gland caused by gallstones. He'd been referred to Josh because he'd developed two cysts, in this case called pseudocysts, in the gland. The cysts were large and very obvious on his ultrasound pictures and CT scans. The position of the cysts meant they were ideally situated for drainage through the stomach, and Josh was confident he could do the procedure through a laparoscope and so avoid a major open operation.

'We still don't understand, Doctor.' Sarah Robinson, his patient's young wife, seemed as confused as her husband by the way they'd been transferred urgently to London. 'We know that Brian's gallstones blocked the drainage from the pancreas and that's why it became inflamed, but we were told that the gallstones passed away on their own. Brian's had hardly any pain these last six weeks.'

'Just the odd bit from time to time,' her husband confirmed. 'Nowhere near what it was before. So why have these cyst things suddenly grown?'

'The pancreas, as you know, makes most of your digestive enzymes,' Josh explained. 'What's happened is that when the gland was inflamed, some of the ducts containing those enzymes broke open and the fluid leaked out and formed the cysts. Often these resolve on their own but because yours haven't they need to be drained.'

'The doctors said they could leak,' Brian Robinson said stoutly.

'And that could be dangerous,' his wife added quickly.

'The pancreatitis could flare up again and Brian could even die.'

'The enzymes in the cysts are very powerful,' Josh confirmed. 'They're capable of dissolving proteins, and proteins are the building blocks of our bodies. I don't believe you're in any immediate danger, but there is the potential for problems, yes.'

'So that's why I'm having this operation on Monday, then?'

Josh nodded. 'I'm going to schedule you for about ten on Monday morning. All going well, that's when we'll do the surgery. I wanted you transferred up here today so we have a few days to do blood tests, along with checks on your nutrition levels. If you need it we'll get special supplementary feeding organised. Also, I want another scan and an X-ray before your surgery. My house officer, Mary, will come to see you soon and she'll explain the tests.'

'My own doctors said they were sending me to you because you're the best one to do the op through a keyhole,' Brian Robinson said. 'With a mini-camera, they said. Seeing me, do you still think that's possible?'

'If you're in agreement, that's what I'll aim for,' Josh told him. 'Keyhole drainage of these cysts is still a relatively new procedure but so far it seems a good, safe method. I'll slide a camera through the wall of your abdomen into your stomach here...' he indicated a three-centimetre line across the top of Brian's abdomen '...then pass a couple of tubes through the skin into the stomach and through the stomach wall directly into the cyst so that the enzymes in the cyst can drain away into the stomach.'

On the CT scan he indicated the dark-looking hollows against the thin, pale wall of the stomach to show what he meant. 'It's straightforward,' he added. 'You'll end up with two, possibly three other small cuts, aside from the longer one for the camera, but you'll find they heal faster than one large wound.'

'The doctors said the old operation for this was a big one and it meant a huge scar,' his patient said.

'There's a small chance at operation that we'll have to convert to a full incision,' Josh warned, 'but things look fairly simple in your case so I doubt if it'll be necessary. With keyhole surgery you can expect to be up and about quickly. By Tuesday you should be walking and by Wednesday you'll be eating normally and we'll be able to transfer you back to your local hospital for a few days.'

'Oh, that's much better than we'd expected.' Sarah squeezed her husband's hand, her expression pleased. 'We thought he'd be in here for weeks. He was in the hospital for five weeks with the pancreatitis. We know everyone there, don't we, Brian? All the staff. They're very nice.'

'I'll see you again tomorrow,' Josh said with a smile. 'If you think of any questions between now and then, save them for me. Otherwise I'll be in Monday morning before surgery.'

He called the consultant who'd referred the new patient. 'I agree that the cysts are suitable to be done through the stomach,' he confirmed once he'd explained his findings. 'When they're that big I like to get on and drain them quickly. We'll do him Monday morning.'

His registrar and house officer, William and Mary, arrived on the ward and he went around with them to check his patient with the fever and the four patients his juniors had admitted so far on their day on call. Apart from an eight-year-old with appendicitis—William was about to take to him to Theatres—and a nineteen-year-old with an inflamed cyst at the base of her back, which William would incise and drain after he'd done the appendix case, there were no outstanding problems needing Josh's input.

Before leaving the ward, he called in to see Mrs Lacy,

now nine days post-operation for bowel obstruction and due to go home the following day. The pathology lab had confirmed that her tumour had been confined to the bowel wall with no spread into the lymph nodes, which meant there was every chance she'd been fully cured by the surgery.

'The nurses will take your staples out in the morning,' he told her, checking her abdomen. 'And the ward clerk will give you an appointment to see me in clinic here so I can check your wound and see how you're getting on.'

'Thank you so much, Mr Allard. You've all been very good.' Mrs Lacy beamed at him. Surprisingly agile so soon after her surgery, she buttoned her nightie then swung her legs over the side of her bed and opened her bedside cabinet. 'I hope you don't mind, but I've made you a little present.'

'A present?' Josh lifted his brows when she passed him a carefully gift-wrapped package. He unwrapped it gently and lifted out a hand-knitted hat and matching navy and cream gloves. 'They're lovely,' he told her. 'Of course I don't mind.'

'For winter,' she told him. 'To keep you warm. One of the nurses mentioned you like skiing so I thought they'd be good for that as well. I knitted the sister a set, too, and I made young Dr William and that nice anaesthetist a pair of nice thick socks each.'

'You have been busy.' Josh was touched. He had proper ski gloves but these new ones, along with the hat, would be useful as spares and when it wasn't so cold. 'Thank you very much.' He shook her hand and reminded her that he'd be seeing her in clinic in six weeks.

William and Mary were still in the doctors' office on the ward. 'I'll be in my office until I finish the dictation from clinic,' he told them. 'After that I'll be on my bleeper at home if anyone needs me. Mary, Brian Robinson needs TED stockings as soon as they can be organised. He's been in hospital for weeks and he's at risk of blood clots. I had a scout around for Bunty to tell her, but she's done a vanishing act.'

'I'll tell her,' Mary said. 'She rushed off somewhere in a hurry a while ago. What time do you want to go around tomorrow?'

'Make it eight.' Josh remembered his plans to take Paige away. 'If we start early we should get away at a reasonable time.'

It was almost eleven by the time he got home. There was a parking space outside the house just big enough for his car, but no sign of Paige's Mini. He wondered where she was parking it. Since she'd arrived to stay he'd only seen it once and that had been the first night when she'd double-parked to unload.

Lights were on downstairs but she wasn't there. He went up to his room but his bed was undisturbed. Frowning, he went to her room, but she wasn't there either. 'Paige?' He checked his study then slowly came back downstairs. 'Paige, where are you?'

'Here! I'm here.' He heard thumping at the inner door and there was a cool blast of night air as she let herself in from outside. 'You're home!' she exclaimed, her cheeks pink as if she'd been hurrying, her eyes very wide and very green. 'Already. How on earth did you beat me back?'

'Who knows?' He held the door open for her to come in then shut it behind her. 'I don't even want to think about it.'

'I've been scoffing biscuits.' She undid her coat and shed it, then clutched her stomach dramatically. 'Chocolate digestives. Dozens of them. Ugh! I feel sick.'

'I'm not surprised,' he observed dryly. 'You only had dinner a couple of hours ago.' Automatically he'd bent and picked up the coat she'd discarded, but when he straightened and saw her knowing smile he realised what he'd done. He pulled a face. 'Next time I'm going to choose a tidy floozy.'

'I dropped it deliberately to see what you'd do,' she said, laughing, her stomach pains apparently forgotten as she danced away from his seeking hands.

'But I know how to slow you down,' she teased. 'Now this.' She shed her jumper on the bottom step of the stairs. 'Pick it up, Josh. You know you mustn't leave the house messy anywhere.'

'Menace!' He collected the jumper and reached for her with his free hand. 'Come here.'

'Not yet.' Ahead of him again, she laughed at him as she pulled her shirt over her head, leaving her lovely breasts bare to his hungry gaze. While he stopped, entranced, she dropped the garment on the floor and skipped away.

He scrunched up her shirt and held it to his face. Still warm from her body, the soft cotton was scented with Paige, and the perfume aroused him unbearably. He followed her more slowly then, letting her stay ahead of him, collecting her jeans and her underwear as she discarded them, until they reached his bedroom and she was naked on his bed, waiting for him.

Letting her clothes drop carelessly to the floor, he went after her.

'I like Bunty,' she told him languidly later when she lay against him in the bath. 'She's funny.'

'Bunty...?' He'd been lazily soaping her breasts with a sponge but now his hands stilled. 'What are you talking about? How do you know Bunty?'

Paige had piled her hair on top of her head with a clip, and when she swivelled around and looked up at him the bunched strands above the clip tickled his face. 'It was Bunty's chocolate digestives I've been eating. Didn't you send her to show me the way out?'

'I have no idea what you're talking about.'

'Bunty,' she said. 'Bunty from your ward. She came and got me from your office then plied me with chocolate biscuits. Bunty, the sister on your ward. The one who's known you since—'

'Paige, I know who Bunty is.' Wondering why he hadn't predicted that the charge nurse would investigate his barred office door more thoroughly, particularly when she'd been so conspicuously absent from the ward, Josh sighed. 'She's a nosy woman,' he said softly. 'Did she harass you?'

'She just wanted to know who I was.' She settled back against him again, wiggling her luscious bottom into the gap between his thighs as she made herself comfortable. With one hand she retrieved the soap he'd discarded and began to spread suds around his right knee where it rose beside hers. 'She's been trying to find a wife for you, too. Matchmaking's her hobby. Now her children are married off she's getting empty-nesty. She'd decided to make you her new project, but then someone told her about me taking you away from the wedding and she wanted to know whether she was wasting her time.'

'Did she indeed?' Josh rolled his eyes. 'What did you say?'

'I said I wanted to find you a wife, too. We've decided to pool our resources.'

Josh winced. The thought of Bunty and Paige pooled against him struck him as little short of horrifying. Alone each was alarming enough, but together...? Even if he'd been capable of thinking of any woman but Paige right now—which, with her body warm and soft and close against him like this he definitely wasn't and he couldn't even imagine a time when he might be—the idea of Paige and Bunty together would still have given him nightmares. He took the soap out of her grip. 'Paige, I don't want anyone else.'

'Of course you do,' she said briskly. 'You want to settle down.'

Slowly, very slowly, he began to lather her breasts again. 'What about you?'

'There's no "what about you".' The continued briskness of her tone suggested that any argument with her on that would prove futile. 'I'm not right for you,' she said crisply, 'and you know you wouldn't look twice at me even if you thought I was.'

'I'd look twice,' he said softly. He touched the side of her neck with his tongue, liking the feeling of her flesh stiffening beneath his palms. 'I'd look dozens of times.'

'Nevertheless, I think it's very important not to miss this opportunity,' she countered, her voice rising with a gratifyingly breathless catch which suggested that his hands might be having as much of an impact on her senses as she was on his. 'Bunty and I will make a great pair.'

'You're trying to give me nightmares.'

'I'm serious.' But she laughed. 'She's going to introduce me to one of the women she's got in mind. Since I know you so well Bunty thinks I should have the final say.'

Sure now that she was teasing him, Josh relaxed. He released the soap and brought both hands up to part her thighs. 'If you ever want to make it out of this bath,' he murmured gruffly, 'stop wiggling that bottom.'

Bunty greeted him with an expectant smile when Josh arrived on the ward the next morning for his round. 'Hi, Josh!'

'It's Saturday,' Josh said flatly, 'and you were on late last night.' Bunty normally worked regular hours rather than the shifts the other nurses covered. 'Why are you still here?'

'Four nurses off on study leave,' she said brightly.

'We're all chipping in.' She collected her notebook. 'I do like Paige.'

'Lovely, isn't she?' He sent her a deliberately bland smile. 'Where are the others?'

'William's in Casualty and he'll be here in five minutes,' she told him. 'The girls,' she added, meaning Mary and the medical student currently assigned to his team, 'are taking blood from Brian Robinson for the tests you ordered. They won't be long. Mrs Lacy's just gone home. She said you'd already said goodbye last night so when her neighbour arrived early to pick her up I let her go. So, Josh, Paige was telling me how keen you are to have children.'

'Paige tends to let her imagination run away with her.' Josh extracted a set of case notes from the cabinet beside them. 'Have the psychiatrists been to see Mr Jenner yet?' he asked, referring to a man who'd been admitted under his care with alcohol-related inflammation of the pancreas.

'They're coming again this morning,' said Bunty. 'They're going to refer him to a treatment programme. Do you think Paige is still in love with David?'

Josh looked up sharply. 'What?'

'Well, she did go out with him and she does talk about him very fondly.' Bunty looked thoughtful. 'If she is, it might explain why she isn't interested in you. You're quite a catch, Josh. For any woman. And Paige obviously cares for you. But at the same time she wants to find you a wife—'

'Bunty, for the last time, I don't need any help,' he interrupted wearily, slamming shut the notes he still held. 'And if you involve Paige in any of your mad schemes I swear I'll strangle you.' He registered her startled look and relaxed a little. 'Good,' he said heavily. 'At least we understand each other now. Let's get started. William can catch us up when he's finished in Cas.' He headed towards the first cubicle at the end of the ward. 'How's Benjamin, by the way?' Bunty had asked him about her grandson's sore throat and fever the day before.

'The GP says it's tonsillitis again,' she told him, bustling alongside him. 'Poor little mite. His father had it at the same age, only in those days they used to whip them out straight away and he only had to put up with a couple of bouts. Josh, we could afford to give them the money to have it done privately if we thought he needed the operation. What do you think?'

'Talk to one of the ENT surgeons,' Josh advised. 'They won't mind you asking.' He knew how concerned she'd been about the child, but tonsils weren't his field and he wasn't up with current thinking on the procedure. 'I suspect they only operate now in severe cases where the children are losing too much school time with infections.'

The traffic was unexpectedly light, leaving London later that morning, and the drive to the coast didn't take as long as Josh had expected. Paige was full of enthusiasm for the area. Inwardly, he'd anticipated seeing little of the area outside the glorious sea and countryside views from their suite, but Paige was having none of that. She dragged him outside and down to the windswept beach and threw pebbles at him when he tried to persuade her back to bed.

'Living in London's turned you lazy,' she cried, dancing ahead, shoes and socks dangling from her hands, her small pink feet splashing through what he knew must be icy shallows. 'You could have had sex at home. You're here for the fresh air!'

So he found himself forced to go walking—and walking, he discovered, with Paige, once she had her shoes and socks back on, didn't mean a civilised stroll to the village pub but a full expedition involving cross-country hiking and scaling of cliffs.

'It wasn't a *cliff*,' she scoffed, when they lay sprawled

and panting at the top and he finally muttered a vague complaint. 'It was a hillock. City boy.'

He rolled his eyes. He enjoyed exercise, only he still didn't see traipsing through the countryside as being preferable to spending a long afternoon in bed with Paige. 'It's going to be dark in half an hour,' he observed. 'I'm starving and you've brought us miles from the hotel without a map. Any ideas, country girl?'

'Back down the hillock then a brisk run along the beach. That way we can't possibly get lost.'

Josh sat up. 'If we're climbing down again, why did we come up?'

'Because it was there?' She laughed when he made a threatening move towards her. 'No tickles,' she screamed when he went for her feet. 'Josh, no! We have to get down before it gets dark.'

'We're hitchhiking.' Instead of tickling her, he tugged her up and brushed her down thoroughly, his hands caressing her as much as ridding her clothes of the sand and grass that clung to them. 'I heard a car. The road must be this way.'

A local farmer stopped almost as soon as they stepped out onto the road. On the way to the hotel he answered Paige's barrage of questions about the area and about the two dogs in the back of his Land Rover and about the tides and the local fishing with gentle courtesy, but Josh sensed from the occasional quizzical look that came his way that Paige's enthusiasm was leaving him mildly bemused.

By way of thanks Josh invited him in for a drink, but the older man carefully explained that his wife would be at home with a meal ready and that he wouldn't like to keep her waiting. 'She always does lamb on a Saturday,' he told them. 'I love my lamb.'

'Roasted?' Paige asked. 'With baked potatoes and parsnips?'

'Grilled fillets marinated in her own yoghurt, served with a lime and coriander pesto,' he said smoothly. 'You'll find the food at the hotel very good. Enjoy the rest of your stay.'

'Thanks again.' Josh closed the door with a grin, lifting his hand in a wave as the farmer drove off.

'Lime and coriander pesto?' Paige blinked up at him, obviously startled. 'Did he say *pesto*?'

'And there you were, thinking you'd met a kindred soul,' he teased, unable to resist stealing a brief kiss from her pursed mouth. 'The yokels are a bit different as you get nearer London, Paige. You must get out of your terrible habit of pigeon-holing everyone you meet.'

'I don't pigeon-hole,' she grumbled, turning on him and stomping away, giving him a delicious view of her bottom. 'I'm very open-minded.'

'Just as Bunty's empty-nesty, and I'm an order freak, and the woman you saw in the supermarket had a ticking biological clock.' He laughed at her disgusted expression. 'Face it, Paige. You're a classic pigeon-holer.'

'I'm merely an impartial observer of human nature,' she said stiffly, while they waited for the receptionist to retrieve the key to their room.

'No, you're a biased cataloguer of it,' he countered. Taking the key, he thanked the receptionist, confirmed their reservation for dinner, then prodded Paige ahead of him towards the stairs. 'Stop dawdling,' he chided softly. 'Unless you want to wait until after dinner for sex.'

She raced up, two at a time, leaving him behind.

As their rescuer had predicted, the food in the hotel's restaurant was very good, if overly generous. Josh managed two courses and a mouthful of Paige's dessert, but while he looked on, incredulous, she polished off the rest of the sweet, then the port which followed it, along with both lots of chocolates they were brought.

He took her to bed, and after they'd made love he lay

with his head on her bare, softly rounded stomach, listening to her dinner churning about. 'You're so small,' he said wondrously. 'I can't believe all that food can fit in here.'

'Youth,' she said languidly. 'Everyone always tells me I'll get hideously fat once I hit thirty.'

'Were your parents overweight?'

'Not remotely. And they always ate like me so I'm keeping my fingers crossed. If I really start piling on the weight I might take up jogging.'

'Because you couldn't possibly cut down on your food,' he teased.

'I couldn't.' She appeared shocked by the thought. 'I love my food. Besides, that would be dieting. Everyone knows dieting makes you fatter.'

Then she frowned. She sat up, dislodging his head so that he fell back onto the mattress. 'Josh…would you still think I was sexy if I got fat?'

'Paige, you'd still be sexy if you were twenty stones and covered in boils,' he groaned, pulling her down onto him. 'Come here.'

Next morning after breakfast she demanded another walk and since she'd said something earlier about considering a swim in the sea, he decided that a walk was by far the lesser evil and quickly agreed.

This time they went towards the village. Not finding the prospect of exploring any of the craft shops lining the main street remotely inspiring, Josh retired to the pub with a Sunday paper to read over coffee, leaving Paige to shop on her own.

He was expecting to have to go and find her when it was time to make their way back to the hotel, but she joined him less than an hour later.

'For you,' she told him, passing him a gift-wrapped

package when he returned from the bar with her tea. 'Thank you for a lovely weekend and happy Sunday.'

'Thank you.' Josh regarded the box dubiously. 'What is it?'

'Open it!' She prodded him. 'It's a present. I can't ruin the surprise.'

Inside he found a small, carved, wooden doll. He studied the creature doubtfully. 'Paige...?'

'It's a fertility doll,' she told him eagerly. 'I saw it and I just thought what an absolutely perfect gift for you.'

Given the circumstances, Josh made what he considered a reasonably noncommittal sound, but Paige laughed.

'I know it doesn't go with your house so just put it in your underwear drawer,' she advised merrily. 'Here, give it to me. I'll put it in my bag so you don't have to carry it.' She took the ghastly thing from him and replaced it in its packaging. 'No one has to see it but it'll still be working.'

'Paige, have you thought this through?' he asked gently. 'I mean, I have no objections, but are *you* sure you really want it to be working just now?'

Her puzzled look cleared after a few seconds. 'Oh, I see,' she said slowly, her eyes widening. 'You mean with me? Yes. Yes, you're right.' She took the doll out of her bag again and eyed it doubtfully. 'I mean, I'm obviously protected but if Mother Nature's determined enough...' She pursed her lips. 'What should I do? I can't take it back because she had a sign saying no refunds.'

'I'll keep it as an ornament.' Hideous though he found the doll, Josh didn't want to risk hurting her by seeming too eager to dispose of the thing. 'Away from my underwear. It shouldn't affect my fertility that way.'

'I don't know.' She still looked unsure.

'You could give it to David.'

'Oh, no, I don't think so, Josh.' Not looking at him now, she took a hasty sip of her tea.

Josh tilted his head. 'Why not?'

'They've only just got married,' she said quickly. 'I shouldn't think they'd be wanting children too soon.'

'You could ask him.'

'No, I couldn't.' She looked uncomfortable and he frowned, puzzled by her uncharacteristic unwillingness to look at him openly. 'I couldn't,' she repeated. 'They're still on honeymoon time. They'll want time to get to know each other better before they think about babies.'

Josh remembered Bunty wondering the day before whether Paige was still in love with David. 'Does the thought of David and Louise having children together bother you, Paige?'

'Of course not.'

'Then why don't you think he'd appreciate the doll?'

'I just told you.' But she didn't look at him. 'I think they'll think it's too soon for them yet.'

'So it does bother you?'

'It doesn't,' she insisted, but she seemed to him to be bothered. 'Why would it?' she added.

Because if she was still having trouble accepting that David had married another woman, then knowing that he was having a child with Louise would be final, irrevocable proof that he was lost to her. But he could hardly confront her with that. He'd asked her once about her feelings for his friend and she'd denied being in love with him. She obviously didn't want to talk about it so it was hardly fair of him to probe further. But he was still…curious. 'You seem rather distracted,' he commented.

'Distracted?' She shook her head. 'No.' But she plainly was, her hasty swallowing of her tea utterly out of character when normally she lingered over her drinks long enough for them to turn stone cold before she finished them. 'It's almost one. Will we eat at the hotel before we leave or on the road?'

'Before we leave,' Josh said thoughtfully.

He'd rung ahead to let his parents know he was bringing Paige to visit Tiger, and when they arrived at the house during the afternoon his mother had afternoon tea laid out in the garden.

'Tiger's around the back with your father,' she told him, removing her apron quickly as she came forward with a pleased smile to greet them. 'Hello, Paige.' She kissed Paige's cheek, before kissing Josh. 'We've heard so much about you. It's wonderful to meet you at last.'

'Has Josh talked about me?' Paige asked, sending him a raised-eyebrow look. 'Really?'

'Not Josh so much. David mostly.' Josh's mother smiled up at him, perhaps catching the sharp look he directed at Paige. 'I was at school with his mother, Paige. We know the family very well.'

Josh watched Paige carefully, but apart from a small smile she didn't react particularly to the comment about David. 'How's Tiger been for you?' she asked instead. 'Not too naughty, I hope?'

'We still have to lock up our slippers and socks,' Mrs Allard confessed. 'But apart from that he's a lovely little dog. He had a congenital hip problem, you know. Josh could tell from the way he walked. He had to have his hip replaced but he's fine now. You wouldn't know. Come and see him.'

Josh thought that 'lovely' wasn't a particularly apt word, given that Tiger was a scruffy and rather ugly dog, but he was lively enough, more like a puppy than a full-grown dog in terms of his energy level.

Paige seemed thrilled with his enthusiastic greeting and she was obviously convinced that the way he kept jumping up at her, licking her, was proof that the little dog remembered her. His parents said nothing and Josh refrained from telling her that what she was seeing was Tiger's characteristic greeting for every adult, child, animal or insect who visited the house.

The dog's sole trick was being able to retrieve the little pieces of stick his father liked to throw at him, but Paige was clearly delighted by the skill. 'He's so clever,' she raved, sending the dog spinning about the lawn chasing the sticks she threw. 'I knew he was intelligent. You could tell even when he was a baby.'

'I don't know if he's that intelligent,' Josh's father said doubtfully. 'I haven't been able to train him to chase a ball.'

'He likes sticks.' Paige ruffled his fur happily while they all looked on. 'Trust me, he's very, very intelligent.'

They had tea in the front garden, surrounded by his mother's hydrangeas. 'I'll fetch more of these,' his mother declared after a little while when Paige had demolished the last of her scones. 'You must be hungry.'

'She's not hungry,' Josh assured her. 'She's just a bottomless pit.'

'I'm not bottomless,' Paige protested with a full mouth. 'I've got a bottom.'

'It's barely two hours since lunch,' he observed, electing to delay any discussion of her bottom to a time when his parents weren't observing every exchange intently. 'You ate three courses.'

'But I love scones.'

'And I've plenty left inside.' His mother's reproving look in his direction made Josh's eyes narrow. 'Look at the poor thing, Josh. She's as thin as a rake. She needs her food. Has he been starving you, dear?'

'Of course I haven't been starving her,' he exclaimed, his exasperation as his mother hurried away inside not helped by the triumphant look Paige sent him. 'She's eaten the cupboards bare.'

'Oh, so you're staying with Josh, are you, Paige?' His father looked interested now. 'At the house?'

'Temporarily,' Paige said, after swallowing, Josh saw, the last of her scone. 'Until I find somewhere else to live.'

'So do you have any ideas about modernising the place? Josh hasn't done anything. It needs a woman's touch.'

'It doesn't need a woman,' Josh said impatiently, tired of hearing that every time either his parents came up or he came down to see them. 'What it needs is an architect, a decent builder, a decorator and time to organise them all.'

'No, Josh, your father's absolutely right.' Paige tipped forward on her seat and tapped his father's hand reassuringly. 'It does need a woman's touch. But don't worry. I'm working on that. Where's the bathroom?'

'Turn right inside the door then first on the left.' As Paige skipped away, Josh saw the delighted look on his father's face and groaned. 'Don't,' he warned. 'Don't even think about it.'

CHAPTER SEVEN

'WELL, I think Paige is lovely.' Josh's mother, returning with a fresh plate of her blackcurrant jam and cream scones, had clearly caught his last comment. 'And it's the first time you've brought a girl to meet us in years, Josh. What are we supposed to think?'

'Nothing.' He gave her a speaking look. 'Think nothing. I brought her because she wanted to see Tiger.'

'Josh, you're not a spring chicken any more—'

'I know that.'

'All the others are married—'

'Yes, I have noticed.'

'And if David can settle down—'

'I'll tell you when it's about to happen to me,' he said wearily, acknowledging that it was his own fault he was in this situation. His mother was right. It had been years since he'd brought any woman home to meet them. In fact, he couldn't remember the last time but it had probably been before he'd graduated.

'A girl like Paige would keep you young,' his mother said lightly. 'Stop you from getting too stuffy.'

'I'm not stuffy.'

'You are a bit stuffy,' Paige chimed in, emerging from the house, obviously having caught the last bit of the conversation. 'He tidies up after me,' she told his mother. 'Mmm. More scones.' She took one. 'Lovely.'

'I don't tidy,' Josh said wearily. 'I just pick things up so I don't trip over them later and break my neck.'

'I'm not allowed to use the washing machine.'

'Because you've flooded the laundry twice already,' Josh

protested, rolling his eyes at his parents' laughter. 'I'm worried about the water leaking through the floor. She used one of my best duvets to mop the floor.'

She wrinkled her nose at them. 'See what I mean?'

'They're very good duvets,' his mother said, wiping her eyes. 'He's told us all about them. They were a good buy. He got them in a sale. Usually they're twice the price he paid.'

'I think they're horrible.' Paige rolled her eyes at him now. 'Think of all the poor ducks that were sacrificed just to keep you warm at night. Give me blankets any day.'

Josh blinked. 'I'm sure they don't sacrifice the ducks.'

'Oh, so they just pluck their feathers out, do they?' She took another scone. 'Well, how would you like your feathers pulled out without anaesthetic?'

'I don't have any feathers.'

'Hairs, then. It's the same thing.'

'No, it isn't,' he protested, bemused that she could advance such an absurd argument. 'It isn't the same at all.'

'It is a bit, Josh.' His mother looked worried now. 'Paige, do you really think they just pull them out?'

'I still think they probably sacrifice the birds,' Paige said faintly. 'I mean, how else do they get that many feathers?'

'I expect they probably pick up the shed ones when the birds move about,' his father said sensibly, winking when Josh sent him a relieved look. 'Probably from free-range ducks. Birds shed all the time, you know. With a big flock they could get loads.'

'I hope you're right,' Paige said fervently.

Josh's mother nodded vigorous agreement. 'I wonder how we can find out for sure?'

'Have another scone.' Josh picked up the plate. 'You, too, Paige. You're probably still hungry. After all, you've only eaten three dozen.'

She poked her tongue out at him. 'He's so rude,' she

said to his mother, although she took another of the scones. 'I bet he was a horrible child.'

'He was a very good child really.' His mother eyed him consideringly. 'We never had any problems with him.'

'Really?' Paige eyed him with irritatingly equal consideration. 'Surprising. Lots of girlfriends, I expect, when he got a bit older.'

'Oh, there were always loads of girls fluttering around,' his mother answered. 'Well, there were,' she protested when he sent her a telling look. 'Weren't there, Bill?'

'Aye, there were,' his father pronounced. 'The numbers have dropped off now, mind. If he doesn't choose one soon there might not be any left.'

'On that ghastly note, I think it's time we left,' Josh decreed with a sigh. 'It's going to take us a while in the traffic as it is. Paige—'

'Let me just go and say goodbye to Tiger,' she said quickly, leaving the table. 'I can't leave without doing that.'

'Thanks for the tea,' he said to his mother as she and his father came with him towards the car. 'Any plans for coming to London?'

'I don't think so, Josh. We've not really thought about it lately.' His mother took his arm. 'Perhaps in a few months.'

Josh nodded. 'I spoke to Ted Wainwright and he's happy with your blood pressure, Dad.' When he'd telephoned his mother to arrange to bring Paige to see Tiger, she'd asked worriedly why he thought his father's GP might suddenly change his father's blood-pressure medication. His father tended to be stoical about such things and wasn't the sort to ask questions himself so, before leaving London, Josh had called the other doctor personally.

'He's very pleased with you,' he reassured him. 'The X-ray and blood tests have been fine and the last heart tracing was completely normal. The new pill he's prescribed is simply a milder formulation of the same tablet. Nothing else has changed. How have you been feeling?'

'Not bad,' his father declared stoutly. 'Which was why we had trouble understanding why he'd be changing anything.'

'It's good to know it was nothing to worry about.' Josh's mother hugged his side. 'Thanks for that, Josh. That was kind of you. You haven't forgotten that the girls are having Jessie's and Emily's fifth birthdays here in six weeks, have you? Will you be able to come, do you think, or are you on call that weekend?'

'I haven't forgotten.' He'd marked the date in his diary. 'I'll be here.'

'Bring Paige. The others would all love to meet her.'

'Hmm.' Paige was shutting the gate between the back and front lawns, confining Tiger to the back part of the garden, and Josh watched her thoughtfully as she came towards them. 'I don't know about Paige.' It was true, he reflected. He didn't know about her. He didn't know at all. She was unpredictable. 'I'll think about it.'

William and Mary, along with one of Josh's consultant colleagues and two other registrars, attended his operation on Brian Robinson the next morning. William had assisted with similar procedures several times before with Josh, but for the others it was a first.

'When I was a student I held a retractor once for hours while someone did a roux-en-y,' Mary told him, referring to one of the open operations often used to drain the type of pancreatic cysts their patient had. 'They weren't doing the op like this then.'

'This is becoming far more common now.' Josh nodded for his anaesthetist to begin expanding his patient's stomach with air so he'd have room in which to manipulate his instruments with less risk of accidentally perforating the lower wall of the stomach. 'Most of the research has been done in North America but we're catching up. That's about right, Ned, thanks.' He tested the fullness of the stomach and indicated for the anaesthetist to stop.

With his camera and instruments in place, and using the transmitted pictures on the monitor on the stand in front of him, he carefully manipulated his forceps to grasp the bottom wall of the stomach.

'When I was a registrar, the sort of hospital stays we were looking at for open drainage of these was about ten to fourteen days,' he told the juniors as he pierced the stomach wall. 'These days we're looking at two to three.'

'What about rates of recurrence of the cysts?' one of the other registrars asked. 'Isn't it higher with drainage through the skin?'

'Through the skin, yes,' he agreed. It was possible to drain the cysts with needles through the skin under CT or ultrasound guidance, but they tended to recur. 'It's early days for us with drainage through the stomach like this, but we're hopeful it'll turn out to be a permanent procedure.'

Once he had both cysts drained and samples collected for examination in the laboratory, he withdrew his instruments and the camera and sutured the small incisions closed.

After writing up his findings and the procedure, he wandered through into Recovery where Brian Robinson was already awake. 'No problems,' he told him. 'Everything went very well. How are you feeling?'

'Not bad.' The other man's voice was blurred through the oxygen mask he was wearing. 'My throat is croaky but I'm not in pain. I didn't believe the anaesthetist at first when he said the op was over already.'

'We'll have you out of here by Wednesday,' Josh told him.

Josh's list was a full-day one and they ran late because

he needed to interrupt his elective cases for an emergency abdominal trauma case. By the time the porters wheeled his last patient into the anaesthetic room attached to his theatre it was almost six.

'Nursing overtime,' his scrub nurse tutted at him lightly when she went to scrub. 'You're lucky we like you so much, Josh, or you'd be on your own for this.'

Josh smiled wryly. 'You know I appreciate you more every day, Lisa.' Lisa had been scrubbing for him for two years, but if she and her colleagues had refused to stay he would have had to postpone his last patient, a young man who'd been nil-by-mouth and waiting anxiously all afternoon on one of the medical wards for insertion of a long, sterile feeding line.

The twenty-two-year-old had severe Crohn's disease, a disease where the bowel became inflamed and fragile. His physicians were hoping that resting the bowel would help it recover and he needed intravenous feeding to keep him nourished.

'He's so thin,' Lisa whispered, once the man was anaesthetised and Josh had begun to drape the side of his neck and a tract across his chest where he'd be partly burying the catheter.

'He's a nice lad,' Josh murmured. He accepted the scalpel and swab she had ready for him and made a small incision over one of the veins in the young man's neck. 'He's a sail-maker and a keen yachty. He crewed in the Whitbread two years ago and he's hoping to sail the Fastnet next year.'

'He looks too sick,' Lisa said doubtfully. 'He looks like a spa bath would knock him about, let alone the ocean. Do you think he'll make it?'

'I hope so.' Using a pair of curved forceps, Josh slid ties under the vein to control it. 'We all have to have our dreams, Lisa.'

He glanced up briefly to retrieve a peanut, a swab on a stick, from her trolley and caught her eyes twinkling at him. 'I dream about the kids one day telling me how much they all love my cheesy spaghetti,' the nurse said lightly. 'What do you dream of, Josh?'

Josh smiled. 'Oh, this and that,' he said softly, carefully inserting the catheter into his young patient's vein. 'This and that.'

Paige spent the first two days of the week back in London after their weekend break at the coast finalising her career plans. 'I'm going to take the research job, starting in six weeks and going through to about August,' she told Josh over dinner on Tuesday night. 'I really want to do that. It'll be interesting. Then I'm going to enrol for that computer course I told you about, starting in September.'

'I thought you'd decided you weren't suited for computer work.'

'I have to be sensible,' she proclaimed. 'It's the sensible thing to do.'

'Paige, if it's money you're worried about—'

'It's not.' Standing to clear their plates, she kissed him. 'I've told you before, I don't need a loan. I can afford to do anything I want but it's still important to think of the long term.'

'I don't like thinking of you having to work in a job that doesn't suit you.'

'Oh, I expect I'll enjoy it well enough once I get started,' she trilled, over the sound of the water she was using to rinse the plates and pots before she put them into the dishwasher. 'I usually like most things. I thought I might like to live closer to the college this time so I've been looking at flats around that area.'

'What?'

He must have moved fast because before she'd even

turned around to answer him he was there in the kitchen, shutting off the taps. He took the plates out of her hand and dumped them back into the water. 'What flats?'

'I've been looking at some,' she said faintly, puzzled by his irritated expression. 'An agent showed me through two last night and I've seen one this afternoon. I'm seeing another three tomorrow but I haven't applied for any of the ones so far. They've all been a bit grotty—'

'Paige, you can live here.'

She swallowed. 'Josh, I can't—'

'Why?'

'You know why.'

'Refresh my memory.'

'I can't stay because I just can't.' She didn't understand why he was surprised. She thought she'd made her feelings clear enough already. 'We both know this is a temporary arrangement.'

'Don't you like it here?'

'Of course I like it.' The question was absurd. 'I love it. That's the whole point. I don't want to love it too much. I don't want to love *you*.'

'For heaven's sake, Paige.' Josh braced his hands against the sink and lowered his head. 'This is ridiculous. Would loving me be the worst thing that could happen to you?'

'It wouldn't be bad,' she said hurriedly. 'Of course it wouldn't be bad. It just wouldn't work.'

He might be enjoying her company now but that wouldn't last. David had told her often enough how impossible she was to live with, and Josh had made his irritation obvious already over the washing machine and the toast crumbs. He'd just grow more and more annoyed by her foibles until he was utterly sick of her. She knew it. She just knew it.

'At least, it wouldn't work for long,' she said firmly. 'And I'd rather not put myself through that.' Even though she was making it her task to find a wife for him, she knew it would still be painful, seeing him with another woman. 'And breaking up can be awkward when you live together,' she added lamely. 'I know. I've been through that with David.'

'*David,*' he repeated, sounding exasperated suddenly. 'David. Paige, it's always David with you.'

She blinked. 'No, it's not.'

'You're fixated.' He ignored her shaking head and faint murmurs of denial. 'You're obsessed with him,' he declared. 'If you think about him even half as much as you talk about him, you must be.'

'No, I'm not.'

'What's David got that I haven't?' he demanded. 'Hmm, Paige? Why can't I give you what you want from David?'

'I don't want David.'

'He's married to Louise.'

'I'm very happy for him.'

'Not happy enough to come to his engagement party. Not happy enough to make it to the wedding in time to tell him and his bride how happy you are.'

'I wasn't…well enough for the engagement party. And I tried to get to the wedding—'

'How could you possibly have been that late accidentally?'

'I tried to get there,' she protested, fighting to overcome the sudden, dismaying prickling of tears behind her eyes as she remembered that day. 'I tried to. I really tried.'

'So how could you be so late?'

'Because I went to the cemetery.' Her whole body had started shaking. 'It was…the six-month anniversary of Dad… I went to the cemetery. To see him. I just wanted to put the flowers there but then I was…crying.'

Like she was crying now, the tears she'd been trying to fight suddenly pouring down her face and dripping from her chin then her hands when she lifted them to wipe the wetness away. 'I knew I had to hurry but...I couldn't. I just sat there. For hours. Crying. And then by the time I got home and got myself cleaned up...it was so late. I'm sorry, Josh, I didn't mean to be late. I didn't mean to miss the wedding. I wanted to see him. I wanted to be there.'

He muttered a soft curse. 'Paige, I'm sorry.' He took her in his arms and she felt his arms smoothing her back. 'I'm so sorry. You don't have to apologise. Not to me. I was wrong. I'm sorry. It just seemed to make so much sense.'

'When I was late...when I came here,' she sobbed softly, 'it was the same thing. I went past the cemetery on my way out, just to say goodbye to Mum and Dad...to explain about coming to London...and then...I just couldn't leave. I stayed there all night and then in the morning I just sat and talked to them and it was ages before I was ready to go. I'm sorry. I must seem mad to you. It's just...Josh, I'm mostly all right now, really I am...but...it's been so hard.'

'Oh, Paige.' She looked up at him and he started wiping her tears away with his thumbs. 'I'm the one who's sorry. I didn't understand.'

'I've been a bit of a mess,' she confessed, rubbing at her face with her fists. 'Well, more than a *bit* of a mess.'

'You've seemed so bright lately.'

'I am bright. Mostly I'm fine. Mostly I'm back to my normal self. But...sometimes I still cry for no reason. I remember things and I get sad. Everyone says that's normal. People say it'll fade in time and I know it will. But it's not gone yet. Not completely.'

'Is there anything I can do?'

'You're doing everything perfectly already.' She wiped her eyes again, with the heels of her hands this time. 'I was just thinking before about how much they would have liked you if they'd met you and that made me weepy again. But I'm all right now.'

'Only I'm frustrating you by trying to stop you from doing what you want,' he said gently. 'You want to leave and, instead of offering to help you find somewhere, I'm arguing with you.'

'I don't *want* to leave,' she whispered. 'I just have to leave. It's best. I'm probably very vulnerable to you at the moment, Josh. Leaving now will make everything easier in the long run. We don't have to stop the sex right away,' she added quickly. 'At least, not unless you want to or until you find someone else, because in the meantime I seem to be managing that all right. I just don't think it's a good idea to keep living too closely with you here.'

But he was frowning at her. 'Can't we do it the other way, Paige? What if you just live here the way you lived with David? Until September. Until you start your computer course. Until you're back on your feet again properly.'

She shook her head. 'Josh, I've told you—'

'No, I mean now,' he interrupted. 'From now. From *before* this gets beyond sex for you, Paige.'

She frowned. 'You mean, instead of moving out I stay, but we stop sleeping together?'

'We'll be platonic housemates,' he agreed.

Paige was confused. 'I don't understand why you want me to stay.'

'The thought of letting you loose on the world makes me shudder,' he replied gently.

'David used to say something like that.' She saw his face darken and added hastily, 'Josh, I really like the sex.'

He smiled. 'So do I, silly woman. You know that. But I'm worried about you living alone now. If something has to go, it should be that first.'

'What about the tidy thing?' she protested, unconvinced. 'What about me flooding the laundry? Josh, you know you don't really want me here. Think of yourself.'

'If you get too bad I'll evict you, but in the meantime you've a decent place to stay rather than some cold, dingy flat. I don't want to think of you somewhere like that.'

She hesitated. 'I won't stay if you won't let me pay rent.'

He looked about to argue but, perhaps interpreting her determined expression accurately, he simply named a sum which correlated roughly with the minimum she'd been expecting to pay. 'Including food and bills.'

'You're underselling,' she warned when he said that. 'Remember how much I eat.'

'I'll live with it.'

Although it would be hard to stop wanting him, it would be a relief not to have to find somewhere else to live immediately. 'Will you promise to be quite horrible to me?'

'As horrible as is humanely possible.'

'And even if I get really…well, excited and demand sex, you promise you'll refuse.'

He smiled. 'Scout's honour.'

'Even if I take off my clothes and jump on you in bed?'

He looked impatient. 'Paige, be reasonable.'

'OK. OK.' She was prepared to concede that that might be an excessive demand. 'Josh, you don't get anything out of this.'

'I get the warm reward of knowing I'm sheltering a poor waif.'

'Actually, I think I do know the best way to pay you back,' Paige said slowly. 'If you'll let me. Agree to this matchmaking thing, Josh. Stop fighting about it and give me a chance. Promise me you'll meet any women Bunty and I decide on.'

He lifted his eyes to the ceiling. 'You're making that part of our bargain?'

She nodded. 'I am.'

For a few minutes he simply looked at her, but finally he muttered, 'One woman. One date. No more.'

'One date,' Paige agreed.

Her face still felt hot and sticky from her tears. She turned away from him and sluiced herself with cold water directly from the tap then dabbed herself dry with the tails of her shirt. 'No peeking,' she warned, when she saw he was eyeing the part of her midriff she'd bared by lifting the shirt to her face with definite speculation. 'We've got a bargain now.'

'Starting nine o'clock tomorrow morning,' he agreed, studying her breasts.

'Starting now,' she countered with a smile, crossing her arms to conceal her body's reaction to him. 'Josh, it's very kind of you to ask me to stay but this is going to be hard for me. Please, don't make it any more difficult than it needs to be.'

He made a small sound of what sounded like disgust. 'Hard for *you*, Paige? That's a joke, is it?' He gave her a brief, exasperated look, swivelled around and stalked out.

But it was hard for her. Very hard, she decided two nights later as she sat in his study, staring at a photograph of him sitting on a beach. She'd gone more than four years without sex, happy with the thought that she wasn't missing anything particularly startling, but now she'd discovered it again and found it wonderful and definitely startling and it wasn't easy to give it up. The only thing keeping her strong was reminding herself repeatedly that by ending that part of her relationship with Josh she was protecting herself from inevitable and catastrophic heartache.

She heard his key in the lock downstairs and a few moments later his steps on the stairs. 'I'm in here,' she called, looking up. 'In the study.' When he came to the door she smiled. 'Hi!'

'Hi.' Still holding his briefcase, he came towards her and swivelled his head to see what she was looking at. 'South of France,' he said slowly. 'Summer...three or maybe four years ago. Having fun?'

'Great fun,' she confirmed, flipping back a page. 'I like being nosy. Who's this?' Every photograph showed a laughing blonde girl sitting, then running, then eating an ice cream on what looked like the same beach. 'Was she your girlfriend?'

He smiled. 'Jealous?'

'Curious.' She studied the picture. 'If this was three or four years ago then it was when I knew you before. I didn't know you were seeing anyone seriously then. She looks nice.'

'She is nice. It's my sister, Jenny. Jenny's the youngest in the family. If you turn over the next one...' he crouched easily beside her and did just that '...you'll see Mum. And Dad. And these are two of my brothers, Mark and Blaire, and Blaire's first baby. My other sister Claire and one of her daughters, Jessie.'

'She's cute,' Paige exclaimed. 'Look at those curls.'

'She was only just starting to walk then. Now she's a real terror.'

He turned over the next few pages to the end of the album. 'I thought there was a good one of one of my other nieces, Emma, here, but perhaps that's in another album. Mum and Dad leased a villa near Antibes for two months and I flew out for a couple of weeks.'

'I was a bit jealous,' Paige said slowly, turning the pages back to the one showing his sister Jenny. 'Strange, isn't it? I think it's because she looked so nice and bright. She looks like the sort of woman who'd make you happy. You know, in those two years I stayed with David, all the women I saw you with were blonde. Whatever happened to Melinda?'

'Melinda?' He looked thoughtful. 'I haven't seen Melinda lately. She took an orthopaedic job at Liverpool and we lost touch. I wonder what she's doing these days. She was a good surgeon.'

'I thought she was awful,' Paige said with a shudder. 'You men are so pathetic,' she added, when she saw her words had puzzled him. 'You only see the surface things like blonde hair and big boobs. David fancied her, too. He thought she was fantastic.'

'Melinda was all right.'

'She was rude,' Paige said vehemently. 'The way she was all over you that night you came for dinner at David's made me sick. She practically had her hands down your pants! Why did she even bother coming to eat? I thought to myself. It was revoltingly obvious she'd much rather be in bed with you. If I hadn't been so embarrassed I'd have offered you the use of my bed for half an hour to settle her down.'

Josh laughed, but she rounded on him. 'It wasn't funny,' she insisted. 'I was worried silly after that night that you'd do something stupid, like marrying her.'

'I don't remember anything about this dinner.'

'I'm not surprised,' she said sharply. 'She kept refilling the wine and swapping drinks to keep yours full. You ended up with three times as much as anybody else. When the cab came we had to pour you into it.'

'But Melinda and I never spent a night together. We were colleagues—'

'You were a lot more than colleagues that night,' Paige interrupted. 'You may not remember the details but if you managed to get out of that cab fully clothed I'd be very surprised. She was wrapped around you like a blanket when it drove off. David was wishing it was him in there with her.'

Josh's eyes narrowed. 'Was that why you didn't like her? Because David did?'

'I didn't like her,' Paige said stiffly, 'because I was so

nervous about you bringing her to meet us when you'd never brought any girl before that I spent two days cleaning and planning my menu and cooking so everything would be nice for her. Only when she arrived she gave me a sour look, dumped her horrible furry coat on me and never sent another word in my direction except to tell me that my spinach soup was bland, my hand-made chocolate mousse wasn't as good as a Sainsbury's one and did I have any crisps because she was simply dying for crisps.'

'And did you?' Josh asked with a profoundly irritating grin. 'Have any?'

'Of course I didn't.' Paige scowled at him. 'If I'd kept crisps in the house I'd have eaten them already. And David had had too much to drink by then so I had to get on my bike and go down to the High Road. In the dark. And in the rain. I'd spent ages doing my hair and that was ruined.

'Then when I finally got back with them no one even noticed I'd been gone, and David was mooning about, making cow eyes at Melinda, and you were halfway to being drunk out of your brain and the ghastly woman only ate two of the blasted crisps I'd gone to so much trouble for and the rest spilled on the floor when she tried to sit on top of you. And I didn't even get a thank you.'

'I wish I could remember that night.' He was laughing again. 'It sounds hilarious.'

'It was a nightmare. I'm never having another dinner party as long as I live. Oh, and I remember something else. I bought a new dress for that night and it got caught in my bike chain when I went to get the crisps. It had this little bodice thing.' She spread her fingers across her chest to show what she meant by the narrow bodice. 'Velvet. It tore from the skirt bit right up so that the whole bodice ended up hanging loose. Lucky I only bought it from a charity shop because I had to use it for rags after that.'

'Velvet.' Josh had stopped laughing and now he was

looking thoughtful again. 'Wait a minute. I remember that dress. It was black.'

Paige frowned. 'I only wore it that night. If you don't remember Melinda, how can you remember what I was wearing?'

'Because you didn't have a bra on.'

'I hardly ever wear one,' she said sharply. 'I'm not big enough to need one. Josh—'

'It was soft and low cut and every time you leaned forward I could see right down your front,' he said slowly.

'Josh!' He was still crouched on the floor beside her, and she slapped his suit-covered arm. 'How disgusting. Why didn't you say something? I could have changed.'

His eyes were very blue. 'You're kidding, right?'

'You mean you… Were you leering at my breasts?'

'Most of the night,' he said evenly. 'Until for some reason you suddenly walked in wearing jeans and a jumper, so I only had your bottom to look at and I had to imagine the top bit again. I wondered if David had said something to you about the dress.'

'He wouldn't have noticed me,' she said faintly. 'Not with someone like Melinda there. I changed into jeans when I got back from buying the crisps after I had the accident on the bike.'

'I probably knew what Melinda was up to with the drinks and didn't care. Getting drunk would have seemed a painless way of keeping my mind off your breasts.'

Paige sent him a bewildered look. 'But I still don't understand. You're a doctor, Josh. By then you must have seen thousands of breasts. Why on earth would you feel the need to distract yourself from my little ones?'

CHAPTER EIGHT

'PAIGE...?' Josh stared back at her, looking bemused himself. '*Why would I need to distract myself from your breasts?* Is that a serious question?'

'Of course it's a serious question.' She looked at him blankly, utterly sincere. 'You had the gorgeous Melinda crawling all over you, practically shoving her chest in your face, and all you remember is my dress? That's pretty strange, Josh.'

'Do you remember what I was wearing that night?'

'Black suit, white shirt with a button-down collar, striped tie with red and grey in it—only you took the tie off after an hour or so,' she said promptly. 'Black shoes, but you took them off and you had nice thick socks. And you had your briefcase. You'd been held up at work, operating on someone who'd been in an accident, and you hadn't had time to go home and change.'

'And Melinda?'

'I don't know.' She shook her head vaguely. 'I'd need to think about it. Something tight.'

'David?'

'I don't remember.'

He held her eyes for a few taut seconds then abruptly levered himself up and away from her. 'I need to get out of this suit,' he said heavily. 'Shall we go out for dinner?'

Paige folded the album closed and scrambled up, leaving it on the floor. 'I bought pasta. There're loads of vegetables there and some cream to make a sauce.'

'Give me ten minutes to have a shower and I'll make it,' he called. 'Oh, and David and Louise are back.' His head came back around the corner of the door to his bedroom, his eyes suddenly narrow. 'They flew in this morning and David rang me at work. He's asked me for dinner next Saturday. Interested in coming?'

'I was planning to drive up to Malton tomorrow.' Much as she'd love to see David and his new bride, she still had urgent things she needed to organise. 'I want to go though the house and put personal things in storage. I was going to speak to an agent about getting it let.'

'Couldn't you be back by next Saturday?'

'I thought I'd stay till the week after. That way I can tidy the garden a bit as well.'

'I'll change dinner to the week after, then.'

'Josh, you can still go next week,' she protested. 'It's not as if you need me there as well.'

But his face had hardened. 'You'll have to face them sooner or later, Paige.'

She frowned. 'I know that—' But he'd already retreated into the bedroom. She heard the sound of the shower starting and since she was already spending hours each day trying not to think about him naked she decided it was best not to pursue him.

After dinner Josh put everything in the dishwasher, murmured something about needing to do some paperwork, then retired to his study.

Paige watched television forlornly for an hour or so until her craving for something sweet grew too strong to ignore. On her first day, staying with Josh, she'd discovered that his local café sold exquisite pastries and cakes so she collected her coat and jogged down to the corner.

'Two strawberry tarts,' she ordered. 'Oh, and a couple of those little blueberry ones as well.'

'You're late today.' The young man behind the counter

winked at her. 'You didn't come in for your *pain au chocolat.*'

'I didn't have time this morning to stop,' she explained with a smile, surprised he remembered her given how busy the café usually was. 'I was running late for a job interview.'

Josh was coming downstairs just as she let herself back into the house, and Paige put the box behind her back so he wouldn't see it. 'Hi.'

'I didn't hear you go out.'

'Oh, I just…' Her voice faded away and she leaned back on the inner door carefully with her shoulders until it clicked shut.

His face was in shadow but she could feel the intentness of his gaze. 'What are you hiding?'

'Nothing.' She crossed the fingers she was using to hold the box. 'Have you finished your work? I was just going to make a drink. Want me to bring you up a tea?'

'You are hiding something.' He took the last metre or so in one jump, a half-smile on his face. 'Paige? What are you up to?'

'I'm not up to anything.' Laughing now, she swivelled around, hiding the cakes with her body. 'Go away.'

'Show me.'

'No!' She doubled over so he couldn't see, laughing still when he grabbed her shoulders, pulled her back against him and tried to straighten her. 'Stop bullying me,' she shrieked when she realised that she was no match for his strength.

'I'm not bullying you,' he protested, laughing now himself as he forced her up. 'Paige, don't be silly. You'll hurt yourself if you try to fight me. Show me.'

'No!'

'What's in the box?' With humiliating ease he removed her fingers from it and lifted it too high for her to reach it. 'Cakes,' he said, his tone disgusted. 'Five cakes!'

'Five!' she cried. '*Five!* He gave me a free one. I only paid for four.'

'But you've just eaten.'

'Hours ago,' she argued.

'Are these all for you?'

'One's for you. I was going to make supper. It was going to be a special surprise.'

'And now I've ruined it.' Grinning, he passed her back the box. 'Sorry. But, Paige, you know I don't have a sweet tooth. I couldn't possibly eat any of these.'

'That's all right. I'll manage.'

'Of course you will.' He took her cheeks between his hands briefly and smiled down at her. 'That's the scary bit. Do you really have to go tomorrow?'

'There's so much to organise,' she said, nodding.

'It's not going to be easy for you,' he said quietly. 'Not so soon. I'm on call this weekend but if you wait till next Saturday I'll come with you. It might help to have someone else there.'

'Thanks, but I'll be fine.' Her voice had gone husky. 'I feel as if those days at the cemetery purged most of the crying out of me. I'm ready for this. I feel that it's time.'

'You don't want me to come.'

'Of course I don't, Josh.' Her smile felt shattered. 'Part of the reason I'm so keen to go up and do this so soon is to get away from you. I'm not coping with this no sex thing very well.'

'But you wanted this.'

'It was your idea,' she protested. 'I agreed because the only alternative was to move out.' She took his hand and pressed it to her breast. 'But feel that,' she ordered, holding him there. 'See? My heart's going wild and my nipples are permanently erect. You walk past me and it's like my hair stands on end. In between times I seem to be spending my days in some sort of dizzy haze.'

'Do you think it's been easy for me?' His hand was still on her breast, and it curved now, cupping her, making her gasp, while his free hand took the cake box out of her hand and dropped it onto the floor. 'Paige, I close my eyes and you're there and I want you. I can barely think straight.'

'You promised,' she said raggedly, her breath coming faster. 'You promised me you wouldn't do this.'

'Just once more.'

'I really think….' But she couldn't think at all. 'I really, really think that you should let go of my breast now.'

But his thumb slid across her nipple. 'But I really don't think I can,' he said huskily, and she felt his other hand shift to the fastening of her jeans. 'I don't know if I'll ever be able to. Paige, I need to touch you.'

'No.' But she couldn't stop her eyes closing as he pressed her gently back against the door, his hand firmly lowering her zip then sliding between her underwear and her skin. 'Absolutely and categorically not under any circumstances,' she whispered.

He touched her mouth with his, his tongue sliding against her, mimicking the probing movements of his fingers. 'What if I said I'll die if I don't have you now?'

'Then I guess…' She sighed, parting her thighs to ease his access. 'I guess under those circumstances it would be very irresponsible for me to refuse just once…'

Josh woke next morning, remembered what he'd done and groaned. He was alone. Paige, together with the mound of blankets she'd insisted in swathing them in, was gone.

He heaved himself out of bed and pulled on his running gear then went downstairs where he found her note. 'There's a blueberry tart in the fridge if you want one for breakfast,' he read. 'It's a bit squashed but that's your fault for dropping the box. Give David and Louise my love. Be good.'

His mouth tightened as he crumpled the edge of the note. The thought of giving David anything resembling Paige's love made him feel sick, and her advice to be good was sound but profoundly belated.

He hadn't intended making love to her again so soon, and the thought that he'd taken advantage of her grief and need for comfort again to coax her into bed appalled him.

Not that she'd been unwilling, he conceded. In fact, even thinking about how responsive Paige was to his touch had the power to arouse him violently, and making love to her was invariably powerfully moving in a way he'd never experienced before or even imagined could be possible.

But when she'd broken down in tears about her parents' deaths he'd begun to understood how emotionally vulnerable she still was. He could no longer kid himself that her responsiveness to him was a product of any feelings for him beyond the sexual attraction they'd always felt and her need now to be close to another human being.

So he'd been determined to keep his hands off her—at least until she was well enough over her grief so that he would know she was consenting to him out of genuine want rather than the yearning for physical comfort and consolation.

His clinic that morning was heavily overbooked. Most of his appointments were follow-ups, people who'd mostly been recent inpatients at the hospital, but the nurse in charge of Outpatients warned him that he also had twenty fresh referrals from local GPs.

'Your first one will only take a minute,' she told him, indicating the thin top set of case notes on the pile. 'She's a nice young solicitor who's been having gallstone colic. She wants to know if she can have them out, please.'

Josh checked her GP's letter and the enclosed ultrasound report confirming gallstones. One of the clinic nurses had checked her urine and blood pressure and both were fine.

The efficient-looking young woman in his first examining room beamed at him when he introduced himself. 'Monica Redmond,' she said firmly, adjusting her spectacles and then shaking the hand he held out. She answered his questions about her history fluently and confidently. 'Mr Allard, I'd prefer keyhole surgery if possible. I like to wear a bikini so a smaller scar would be better. Is my case suitable for that?''

'There's no reason why not,' Josh assured her. Most of his patients these days asked for the less invasive form of operation. He explained the possible complications and warned her that although laparoscopic surgery meant a shorter stay in hospital and less post-operative discomfort, the risks of complications remained higher than with open surgery. 'Also, if the operation proves difficult we may have to convert to open surgery,' he added. 'It's rare but you should be aware that it's a possibility.'

She nodded. 'Yes, my doctor did discuss that.'

Josh examined her. He checked her hands and eyes for signs of jaundice and anaemia and her abdomen for the size of her liver and for tenderness or swelling over her gall bladder. 'You're very tanned,' he commented.

'Florida sun.' She smiled. 'My partner and I are just back from two weeks away. We were having a good time until my gallstones played up. I was glad I was due for this appointment.'

Josh finished examining her abdomen then paused over her lower legs. 'Your left leg's swollen.'

The difference between her legs wasn't conspicuous, but when he pressed with his thumb over her left shin he made a deep imprint and her calf was overly warm. She lifted the leg up fractionally and peered at it. 'It's been stiff since I got back,' she revealed. 'We slept throughout the flight so I assumed I'd had it at a funny angle.'

Josh wasn't so sure. 'Any breathlessness or chest pain?'

'I have been a bit wheezy,' she admitted. 'I put it down to a pollen allergy. Why?'

'I'm worried you might have a blood clot.' He tapped out her lungs then checked them with his stethoscope, but he couldn't hear a wheeze or anything else abnormal. But finding no signs of an embolus in the lungs didn't rule out a thrombus in her leg. 'We need to investigate this,' he told her firmly. 'Blood clots in the legs aren't uncommon after flights, particularly transatlantic ones, and the contraceptive pill you're taking adds a second risk factor.'

She looked concerned but not overly alarmed. 'And the treatment is?'

'Medication for three months to thin your blood and prevent more clots forming or breaking off and travelling to your lung. Your own body will eventually dissolve the clot.'

'Will I need to stay in hospital?'

'Three to four days on a medical ward until the medication has time to take full effect,' he confirmed. 'Will a few days in hospital cause problems with your work?'

'Not any I can't handle,' she assured him with a brisk smile. 'I'm more concerned about my gallstones. Will this delay my operation?'

'If you need blood thinners then surgery will have to be delayed until the course is finished, yes,' he admitted. 'Elective surgery's too risky otherwise.'

'But best I sort this out first.' She met his gaze steadily. 'If this is a clot and it spreads to my lung then that can be fatal, can't it?'

'That's the reason it's important to get on and treat it immediately,' Josh confirmed, reassured by the brisk matter-of-factness of her manner that she could handle complete frankness.

While she dressed, he explained his suspicions directly to the radiologist on call. 'Send Ms Redmond straight to

the department, Josh,' the other doctor instructed. 'I'll ultrasound her leg immediately. Can she walk or will she
need a wheelchair and porter?'

'No, she's fit and well,' Josh assured him. 'Thanks.'

The radiologist rang him twenty minutes later, catching
him between cases. 'Josh, you were right,' he announced.
'The clot's extensive. I've spoken to Nuclear Medicine and
they can fit in a lung scan at three.'

'I'll tell the physicians,' said Josh. Hospital protocol dic-
tated that people with blood clots of Ms Redmond's type
were admitted to medical rather than surgical beds and Josh
arranged for her care to be transferred to one of the hospital's senior medical doctors.

Directly after his clinic he went up to the medical ward
to see her. Her oxygen mask and the drip in her arm attached to the blood-thinning infusion didn't seem to be
slowing her down on her laptop, although she put the computer aside with a warm smile when he came in.

He glanced though the chest X-ray and blood tests the
medical house officer had passed him outside. 'Your X-
ray's fine but one of the blood tests the medical house officer's just done suggests the oxygen level in your blood
isn't as high as it should be,' he explained. 'The lung scan
this afternoon will tell your new doctors if clot has already
spread there.'

'I understand.' She nodded. 'I'm told you might have
saved my life, Mr Allard. I wasn't at all worried about my
leg so it's very lucky for me that I came to see you today.'

Josh didn't even want to think about what could have
happened if she hadn't. Leg clots didn't always spread but
her oxygen levels were alarming enough to suggest that
hers was the sort that did.

'I'll schedule your gall-bladder surgery for two weeks
after your treatment's due to finish,' he announced. They'd
need to take special precautions then to minimise her risk

of developing more blood clots because surgery, along with flying and oral contraceptives, was another risk factor in their development, but he didn't foresee any problems otherwise. 'It's probably best to avoid fat until then.'

She smiled again. 'Considering one piece of fried chicken in Florida gave me forty-eight hours of pain, I'm off fat permanently,' she said lightly. 'Thanks again for your help, Mr Allard.'

Josh nodded. 'You're very welcome. All the best.'

He'd arranged to meet William and Mary in the doctors' office on his own ward to do a round, but since neither of his juniors were there yet he used the telephone to call David at his surgery.

His friend sounded pleased to hear from him. 'All on for next Saturday, then?'

'Dave, I'm going to have to opt out.' Still perturbed by Paige's reaction to David's marriage, and wanting time to consider that and the possible consequences of it, he'd not yet told the other man that Paige was staying with him. 'How about the Saturday after?'

'No problem.' David chuckled. 'Shame you can't make it next week, though, because one of Louise's girlfriends was coming, too. Remember her chief bridesmaid, Catherine?'

Josh grimaced. 'Don't do this to me.'

'Hey!' David laughed again. 'Just trying to help out. I haven't forgotten what you said at the wedding about wanting kids. Catherine's a great girl and, remember, she's a paediatric nurse. She loves kids. Besides, she's gorgeous.' He whistled. 'Really something. Just your type—'

'You're wasting your time.' Josh gritted his teeth. Bunty had been going on at him about the same woman and he had vague memories of the bridesmaid being attractive, but that didn't change anything. 'I'm not interested.'

'You won't say that when you meet her again properly,'

his friend declared confidently. 'We'll see if she can make it the week after as well. Josh, I've got to tell you, marriage is the greatest thing on earth.'

'So you said on your wedding day,' Josh reminded him. 'Only then you were too drunk to talk seriously so I'm glad to hear you say it again.'

He heard someone saying something in the background and then David was back, sounding more urgent now. 'Got to go. Some teenager's fallen off his bike in the high street and sprained his ankle and cut his head open. Sounds like he's bleeding half to death in my waiting room so I'd better pop a few stitches in. See you Saturday week, then.'

William and Mary came dashing up just as he was finishing his conversation with David and they went around the wards. Afterwards, Josh returned to the medical part of the hospital to see Danny Newman, the twenty-two-year-old he'd operated on the day before.

'The feeding line's working perfectly,' the house officer looking after him told Josh. 'We haven't had any problems. He had saline through the line overnight and now we're slowly building up the strength of his TPN. He'll be on full strength by the morning.'

Josh nodded. TPN, or total parenteral nutrition, was the name given to the sterile mixture of fats, carbohydrates and protein in the black bag attached to Danny's new line. 'How are you feeling, Danny?'

'Terrific,' he answered, and Josh admired his spirit because 'terrific' had to be a massive exaggeration, considering the other man looked tired and drawn and was clearly still very ill with his colitis. 'No problems at all,' the younger man added. 'I hardly notice the drip.'

Josh checked his temperature chart, the tubing and the dressing covering the line's insertion site, then drew back, noting with a nod the thick collection of boating magazines and books on Danny's bedside table. 'Planning some heavy reading?'

'Yeah.' The younger man's grin was self-deprecating. 'Two months in a hospital bed's no excuse not to keep up. Things change fast in this field.'

'I know the feeling.' But Josh's return grin was rueful. He was impressed with Danny's dedication but in his situation he doubted whether he'd have had the same drive to keep up with his own journal reading.

'Those stitches will need to stay for five to seven days and I'll be back to check them again in a couple of days,' he told the house officer.

On the following Friday afternoon, at the end of what had proved a long week without Paige, Josh finished his theatre list, did a quick round of the wards with William, then handed over his patients to one of his colleagues for the weekend, before heading north towards the M1, the bag he'd packed the night before already in the back of his car.

He hadn't told Paige he was coming because he suspected she'd try to dissuade him, but he was worried about how she was managing on her own. If he could help, he wanted to.

Traffic was heavy and around Sheffield it slowed it to a crawl, but once he got off the motorway and through York he had a clear run for the last short stretch into Malton. He had Paige's address and he stopped at a pub—there was no shortage—for directions.

The house, a brick cottage set off the road behind a garden which might have been cherished once but clearly had seen better days, was easy enough to find after that. He smiled as he saw the little Mini parked haphazardly alongside the house. There were lights on inside the house and the door was ajar, but when he knocked she didn't answer. He pushed the door open. 'Paige? Are you here?'

'Josh!' She emerged from a room to one side just as he stepped in, her eyes wide in her pale face. 'You're...here!'

'I wanted to make sure you were all right,' he explained, unable to stop himself from inspecting her hungrily, the jeans and jumper she wore clinging close enough to her luscious body to set his heart on fire even if he hadn't had the excuse of more than a week without her.

'I'm fine.' She had a rag in one hand and a china clown in the other, but she crouched and put them on the floor. 'Really fine. Um...' She smoothed her hair. 'I don't know what to say. You've taken my breath away. You must have had a long drive. I've bread if you want me to make you... Or there's a good fish and chip shop—'

'I had a sandwich on the way,' he said dismissively. 'Is there anything I can do?'

'You could help me bring the stuff down from the attic,' she said slowly. 'I've been trying to do it alone but the boxes are heavy.'

'Let me change first.' He'd discarded his jacket and tie during the drive but he was still wearing his suit pants and his shirt. 'My bag's in the car.'

When he came back she showed him into what looked like the main bedroom. 'I'm not using this,' she said, evidently interpreting his quizzical look correctly. 'I'm in my own room. You are staying, aren't you, Josh?'

'I could try a pub.'

'Of course you won't,' she said quickly. 'I didn't mean that. I was just making sure you didn't have any mad idea about driving straight back down again once...'

'Once?' he echoed, when she trailed off.

'Once you saw I was OK,' she finished, with a quick smile.

'I was thinking late Sunday.'

'Great.' She gave a little shrug but to his relief she didn't seem displeased. 'Mmm. Great.'

She left him to change and when he came out she had a ladder erected and was starting to climb up into the attic.

'Leave them,' Josh ordered firmly, lifting her aside. 'I'll do the heavy stuff.'

'Most of it I'm either giving to the charity shops here or throwing out,' she told him eventually when she began sorting through the boxes he'd carried down. The strong scent of mothballs rose from the second one she opened. 'Mum kept everything. Look!' She pulled out a tiny gown. 'This was from my christening.' She burrowed deeper. 'Oh, this whole thing's full of baby clothes and toys.' She pulled out a tiny gym slip. 'My first school uniform.'

'The baby clothes will be good for your own children,' he said quietly. She'd started blinking fast and he put his arm around her. 'They're special. Will you keep them?'

'I think I might.' She sniffed. She looked up at him, her eyes damp and pink, but she didn't cry. 'I've found a nice family who want to come and live here when I've finished,' she said faintly. 'They've two little girls, one and three. They've been living in Wentworth Street but there's not enough garden now the children are getting bigger. When I'm in London it'll be nice to think of people living here again. Thank you for coming, Josh.'

'Even though you told me you didn't want me to?' He smiled. 'I thought you might send me away.'

'Oh, no.' She stepped away from him, looking satisfyingly shocked by the idea. 'I just…well, I just thought I needed some time to get the…sex thing out of my system.'

'And have you?'

'Hardly.' Her eyes had cleared now and she rolled them at him. 'But I've got a plan now. I'm going to try and find a boyfriend.'

CHAPTER NINE

JOSH felt as if all the air had been sucked straight out of his chest. Slowly, he let himself down onto the floor. Keeping his expression as controlled as he could manage, he leaned back against the wall behind him. 'What?'

'A boyfriend.' Paige's smile was slightly off centre, as if she wasn't as sure of herself as she sounded, but she didn't take the words back. 'For sex.'

'Paige—'

'I won't bring him back to the house,' she said quickly. 'At least not often. And me finding a boyfriend would solve all our problems, wouldn't it?'

'How?' His head was spinning. 'How can you possibly think that would begin to solve anything?'

'Firstly,' she started, counting on her fingers, 'he would take care of the sex stuff, meaning we'll be able to stop worrying that we're about to jump into bed together. Secondly, we could double date with the woman Bunty and I pick for you so meeting her won't be as awkward as a blind date might be.' She sent him another slightly shaky smile. 'It's so important to get a good start in these relationships. Number three, when you decide she's the woman of your dreams, if I've got a boyfriend then she won't worry about me staying at your house, meaning I'll have a bit more time to find somewhere else to live while the two of you go through the whole courting ritual thing.'

Josh was shaking his head. 'Paige, there's not going to be any courting thing—'

'Number four.' She waved her hand to stop him and

raised her voice. 'Let me finish, Josh. You're always inter-
rupting. Number four, a boyfriend would be fun.'

'Fun?' He was appalled. If she thought he was going to
stand mildly by while she involved herself with another
man for *fun* then she was in for a shock. 'You can have
fun with me,' he said shortly.

'Your sort of fun's dangerous,' she told him sternly. 'I
knew after what happened last Thursday that I had to come
up with a plan, and this is a brilliant one. Josh, it's your
fault,' she blurted when he simply glared at her. 'You're
just too seriously attractive for me to control myself when
there's no alternative available. At least if I have a boyfriend I'll have someone else to turn to when you…well,
when you…make me want to have sex.'

'When *I*?' he demanded, abrupt disgust at that thought
distracting him from anything else. 'When *I* make you want
to have sex? You mean when you're aroused by *me* you
want to be able to go to another man?'

'Mmm.' The thought disgusted him but Paige didn't
seem perturbed. 'Josh, I know you don't do it deliberately
but sometimes you only have to look at me in a certain
way and I—'

'Do you have someone in mind?'

'In mind?' She blinked at him with a vagueness that was
as infuriating as it was frustrating. 'For what?'

'This boyfriend.'

'Not really.' But she gave him another of her unbalanced
smiles. 'The man in the café near you is sweet. He gave
me an extra blueberry tart the other day. I was wondering
if he gets free cakes.'

Free cakes! Josh sagged, his fury abruptly drained by the
sheer absurd nonsense of it all. 'I can't compete with free
cakes,' he said thickly.

'You're not supposed to compete.' She came forward on

her knees and tapped his cheek with her palm. 'It's all right, Josh. Really. You're supposed to be relieved.'

'I'm not.' He was…numb. He caught her wrist. 'Paige, this is ridiculous.'

'It seems quite sensible to me,' she declared earnestly in a reassuring sort of tone. Only he wasn't reassured in the slightest. 'Besides, eventually I expect I'll start fantasising about him instead of you. I'm sure it will work out fine.'

Josh was equally sure it wouldn't. Or at least that he didn't *want* it to. 'It's immoral.'

'Immoral?' She rocked back on her heels, her face gratifyingly concerned suddenly. 'Do you think so?'

'Of course.'

'You're saying I shouldn't try and find someone just for sex?' she said slowly.

Josh breathed out slowly. 'I am.'

'But men do it all the time.'

'They don't.'

'Yes, they do.' Her green eyes narrowed on his face. 'Don't look at me like that, Josh, because you're no exception. You've had sex with me, remember,' she went on, equally incomprehensibly. 'We both went into this knowing there was no future but you wanted sex. And that's fine because I wanted that, too. But now because I'm a woman openly wanting the same thing you're telling me I'm immoral. That's a double standard.'

Josh took a deep breath. Any discussion about his intentions would only confuse things now so he let her comments pass. 'I'm not saying *you're* immoral,' he pointed out heavily. 'I'm saying sex for sex's sake is. Making love is supposed to be a precious, intimate and emotional exchange. Shouldn't you at least be fond of the man?'

Paige regarded him dubiously. 'Are you saying you've never taken a woman to bed purely for the sex?'

'I'm saying that exactly,' Josh confirmed quietly. 'Of course I am. Yes.'

She looked confused. 'Josh, David used to tell me—'

'Don't quote David's stories at me,' he retorted abruptly. 'He made them up.'

'He said when you were students together—'

'I'm not saying I've been celibate, Paige. I've had relationships with women,' he conceded. 'Obviously none lasted permanently, but neither were they based on sex. My interest in my partners was always sincere.'

'Like your interest in Melinda?'

He winced. 'I hope I didn't do anything to mean I deserve that,' he said heavily. 'But if I did then she would have been one exception. Paige, Melinda and I were colleagues. We worked long hours together for a long time. I wasn't seeing anyone at the time that you and David invited me to dinner, but I expect I still wanted to take a date. I would have had no idea she'd read more into that than I intended.'

'David and I wouldn't have minded if you'd come alone,' she said. 'Honestly, given the way she carried on, I'd have preferred it.'

'It was a long time ago,' he said flatly. He knew he must have taken Melinda that night as a way of concealing his interest in Paige, but he didn't want to go into that now. 'I don't remember everything.'

'And what about me?' A frown creased the flawless skin between her brows. 'Am I…a *relationship*?'

'Of course.' He recognised the irony of the reassurance she was seeking when he felt as if he was the one who needed reassuring. 'Paige, I didn't sleep with you because I wanted sex. I slept with you because I wanted *you*. You the person, not you the body.'

'You liked my bottom,' she countered.

'I *love* your bottom.' His eyes dropped automatically but

with a faintly nervous look in his direction she promptly sat down. 'But your bottom on another woman wouldn't have made me want her instead.'

'I still think it's quite simple. I just have to find a boy-friend I'm fond of but, Josh, you needn't have worried. I was going to do that anyway. I could never sleep with a man I didn't like.'

'Even for free cakes?'

'Even for free cakes.' She beamed. 'It isn't just the cakes—he's sweet.'

Josh scowled. '*Sweet* isn't enough,' he said tightly. 'I thought we'd been through this—'

'I'm teasing,' she gurgled, laughing. 'Heavens. Listen to yourself, Josh. Anyone would think you're jealous.'

'Of course I'm jealous,' he growled.

'But why?' Her lovely green eyes blinked at him with unconcealed astonishment.

'Because I'm not ready to give you up yet.' He was impatient. 'I'm prepared to put up with living with you platonically because I recognise that's what you need at present, but I'm not ready to see you go to another man.'

He wasn't necessarily expecting to swear eternal devotion then, but the sudden angry creasing of her face surprised him. 'You want me to stay around conveniently until you're sick of me,' she said accusingly.

He blinked. 'What?'

'I'm not stupid, Josh.' In an abrupt movement she un-coiled her legs and jumped up, glaring down at him, her hands on her hips. 'You and I both know that if we were still involved then that day would be fast approaching.'

'What day?'

'The day you decide you can't live with me any longer because I've left my…socks on the floor or…crumbs in the kitchen or something just as trivial one time too many,' she retorted. 'Or the day you meet your dream woman, the one who's good enough to bear your children. You'll boot me out fast enough then.'

'That isn't going to happen,' he responded. 'You're talking nonsense—'

'It's the truth,' she insisted, clearly still cross. 'Josh, I've been completely honest about my feelings to you so, please, be honest with me in return. I've told you why I'm worried about spending too much time with you.'

'You're worried about being hurt.'

'Yes.' She met his regard unflinchingly. 'You could hurt me terribly.'

'I don't intend to cause you pain,' he retorted, exasperated. 'Paige, for heaven's sake—'

'What you *intend* doesn't matter,' she cried. 'Josh, there's no future for us.' She looked so sure of herself that he realised he'd get nowhere attempting to argue the point then. 'You're only refusing to admit it because you want to get me into bed now.'

Josh sighed. He rose to his feet, his movements weary as he conceded that although she had his motivation wrong, and although he knew that his desire was despicably selfish, she wasn't wrong about what he wanted. With her eyes almost spitting green sparks at him and her chest lifting with the effort of her enraged breathing, despite knowing how bad coaxing her into his bed had made him feel the last time, the effort of not hauling her against him and kissing away her resistance was taking every ounce of his self-control. 'I'm going to bed.'

She followed him to the door. 'You won't have to be celibate for long, Josh. Bunty and I have found a wife for you.'

'No, Paige.' Josh studied her with what he considered to be creditably mild exasperation. 'There's no point. It's time you and Bunty stopped this insane scheme—'

'It's not insane,' Paige insisted. 'And you should be thankful. You want a wife—'

'Not one chosen by you.'

'It's too late to back out now.'

He stiffened. 'What?'

'It's all organised.' She tilted her little chin up with a determination that made the urge to kiss her senseless almost overwhelming. 'I wasn't going to tell you until I'd had the chance to see her myself but, well, Bunty knows what she's doing. Her name's Catherine. She's a nurse on the children's ward at your hospital. Bunty's told me all about her and she sounds perfect for you.'

Catherine. Josh sighed. 'Louise's bridesmaid.'

'Apparently, you were too busy to have time to talk at the wedding,' Paige told him carefully, nodding. 'Bunty says she's very keen. I was thinking that if I found a boyfriend quite quickly then we could double date.'

He curled his hands into fists to stop himself reaching for her. 'No.'

'You promised.'

'I didn't keep my other promise either,' he pointed out tightly.

'But you would have died otherwise.' She smiled up at him, a sweet, almost shy smile which weakened his resolve terribly. 'So I didn't mind that,' she added huskily. 'I couldn't really. Not when you told me that. But I would mind you not keeping this one.'

He came forward and took her cheeks between his palms, still determined—absolutely determined—not to kiss her but unable to stop himself trying at least a little bit. 'What if I said I might die if you made me meet another woman?'

'I would warn you to be very careful about crying wolf,' she said softly.

'What if I said I thought I might die right now if I didn't kiss you?'

'I would say just one little kiss,' she whispered, going up on tiptoe. 'I would say one little kiss couldn't possibly do any harm.'

He kept his hands off her by sheer strength of will and kissed her softly, letting his tongue just touch her lower lip as lightly as he could manage when every cell in his body wanted to devour the sweet mouth that opened for him so obediently. Slowly, very slowly, he drew back. 'What if I said I thought I might die right now if I didn't see your breasts?'

'I would say you're pushing your luck, Josh Allard.' She gave him a shaky smile and her voice was gratifyingly hoarse. He could see her breasts lifting beneath her jumper again as if the effort of breathing was as hard for her as it had grown for him. 'I would say it's late. I would say that it's time you were in your bed. Alone.'

'This conversation isn't finished.' A quick glance at his watch told him she was right about it being late. It was ten minutes before three in the morning. They'd been talking for hours, and although Paige still looked fresh and alive she was also far too desirable for him to resist her any longer when he was tired after the long day.

Not too tired for her, he conceded dryly, knowing he never would be. But definitely too tired to be able to be sure of his control. 'And we will finish it, Paige,' he warned softly. 'Don't think you're getting everything your own way.'

Paige lasted less than twenty minutes in her own bed. She had been determined, absolutely determined, to stay where she was, but it didn't take long to realise that there was no way she was going to get a wink of sleep without Josh. Not when he was so tempting and so close, and not when it had been more than a week since she'd last touched him or been held in his arms, and certainly not when he'd looked so wonderful tonight and when his goodnight kiss had been so frustratingly restrained and so tender that she'd ached to simply give into her longing and take his hand and lead him to her bed.

One more kiss hadn't done her any harm. Surely one more night together wouldn't hurt?

Taking a bundle of blankets from her bed in case she got cold, she tiptoed to his room. The door was ajar and she opened it softly the rest of the way. She crept over and folded her blankets over the end of the bed, then shed her nightie, tiptoed around and burrowed under the covers. The slow steadiness of his breathing confirmed he was asleep.

Telling herself it was ridiculous to feel forlorn about him being able to sleep calmly without her, she turned carefully onto her side. She wouldn't wake him, she told herself. She would be content with just being close to him.

Only her hand crept out to his bare chest. When he wasn't disturbed, she couldn't stop herself from wriggling just a little bit closer to him. When he still didn't wake she couldn't quite stop herself snuggling just a little bit against him and fitting herself into his side where he lay sprawled on his back.

Only being close to him merely accelerated her heartbeat and made her more alert than she'd been all night, and there was still no obvious prospect of any relief for her frustration. She swore in her head and turned irritably away back to her own side of the bed, her back to where he still slumbered so peacefully. Screwing up her eyes, she mentally recited half-buried sagas she'd been forced to memorise during her school poetry studies, but then she jumped about a foot off the mattress when a warm hand curled around her stomach.

'Mmm.' His murmur was sleep-roughened and warm with approval. 'No nightie. Nice.' He brought her back against him so she could feel he wore nothing himself, his hand lowering to the junction between her thighs to stroke her. 'You're a contrary girl, Paige Connolly.'

'You're too sexy,' she whispered, closing her eyes weakly at the seeking probing of his fingers and the unmistakable response of his body against her buttocks. 'It's your own fault, Josh. You make me think of things I shouldn't be thinking of. But I didn't mean to wake you.'

'I've told you before.' His mouth was warm and seeking at her ear as he caressed her. 'I like you waking me.'

After a little while he slid his hand away from between her thighs. 'Paige, I wasn't going to do this,' he said gruffly. 'You're still vulnerable—'

'Not as vulnerable as I'll make you if you stop now,' Paige growled as menacingly as she could manage when she could barely think. Her hand on his chest, she moved him over onto his back. 'I need you, Josh.' Breathless and eager and desperate for him, she lifted herself and came up onto him, folding herself around him, bracing herself with a spread hand against his chest.

'I couldn't sleep for thinking about you,' she told him urgently. 'I haven't slept properly for days because of thinking about how you feel inside me. Thinking about this. Wanting this.' She rocked forward once, then stopped abruptly, tensing, catching her breath at the exquisite pressure of his body against her. 'Oh.'

'No!' His own breathing ragged now, Josh pulled her down, cradling her against him, caressing her, stroking her back, holding her, while he moved against her himself now, groaning his frustration as she dissolved against him. 'Don't go to sleep.'

'I'm not,' she lied, trying to lift her head, but the effort was too much when her neck felt like heavy jelly. 'I won't.'

'Paige...?' The groan was half laughter, half disbelief, as if he thought she might be teasing him, but she could only curl her hand against his chest in response, her energy so drained she hardly knew herself any more.

'Paige…?' Out of the corner of her mind still working she dimly heard his protest, but the gentle way he was stroking her hair as it lay on his chest lulled her into utter calmness. 'Paige, you know this isn't polite.'

'Do whatever you want.' She waved her fingers at him, too drained to move at all now. 'I don't mind. Sorry.'

When she woke daylight was streaming in between the slats in the room's vertical blinds and she rolled over and smiled at him, feeling light and happy and blissfully refreshed. 'What a beautiful morning.'

'Pity you're not going to see any of it,' he growled. He closed the magazine he'd been reading, slammed it to the floor and reached for her. 'Nuisance.'

'Why?' Paige laughed, wiggling against him deliberately to tease him as he moved over her. 'What's wrong?' she squealed, when he nipped her breast playfully. 'What have I done?'

'Nothing but sleep.' He bit her chin, then her ear. 'Nothing but sleep like a sloth all night.'

'Not all night,' she argued, still laughing, twining her legs around his hips as he surged against her. 'I was awake for the best bit.'

'*Your* best bit.' His expression half-exasperated, he captured her mouth urgently. 'You creep into my bed in the middle of the night. You wake me up. You wiggle that bottom against me and *deliberately* arouse me when I'm determined not to be aroused. Then you take your pleasure before I even get a chance to play, and then you fall asleep. I've been awake all night, Paige. And it's not the first time you've pulled a stunt like that. You need a lesson in staying awake, and you need to learn that once is not enough.'

'You could have gone ahead without me,' she protested,

still laughing despite the pulse-thudding revelation of what he wanted to do with her. 'I told you I didn't mind—'

'Strangely enough, I prefer you conscious.' His hands slid under her buttocks, lifting her against him. 'Minx. Shut up and concentrate.'

Hours and hours later she stretched back, half on, half off the bed, looking backwards towards the window, her hands trailing on the floor. 'I'm still languid,' she said lazily. 'A bit...heavy, I suppose. But not sleepy.' He was still on the bed so she couldn't see him, but she stroked his thigh with her bare foot. 'So, do I finally pass, Josh? I mean, you can't test me much more than that. Do I pass? Hmm?'

When he didn't say anything she prodded him with her foot more firmly, but when he still didn't say anything she swung herself up onto the bed, her smile softening as she saw that he was now sprawled asleep himself.

'Fraud,' she whispered, coming up to crouch on her knees beside him and kissing him so softly she couldn't possibly wake him.

She spent the afternoon sorting through the sewing room and study. She was letting the house furnished, except for the more valuable or sentimental pieces which would go into storage until she had somewhere to put them.

Her week in Malton had reinforced her decision to stay in London. People in the village were warm and friendly and kind, but without her parents it didn't seem like home any more. She couldn't sell the house yet, but one day, perhaps when she had her own family, she thought she might be able to. She'd miss the village and the moors but she wanted to be in London now.

Josh slept until evening. She checked on him from time to time, stroked his cheek or touched his hair, but he didn't stir. Finally she heard the floor creak in the bedroom and then the water being turned on in the shower. She lifted her head and smiled. When the water stopped she put aside the cleaner she'd been using to scrub down the walls in the kitchen and went to see him.

Meaning only to glance into his bedroom on her way past, she suddenly froze, and when he came out of the bathroom a few minutes later she was still there.

'Sorry, I slept so—' His voice behind her started off apologetic but then it turned concerned. 'Paige, what's wrong?'

'I've just realised,' she said slowly. 'I mean, I have *just* realised I spent the whole morning having sex with you on my parents' bed.'

'Is that all right?'

'Oh, they wouldn't have minded,' she said numbly, swinging around. 'They weren't prudish. They were always very open in their own affection for each other.'

'So is there any problem?'

'There isn't one at all.' She smiled at him, a smile of pure relief. 'You see, I didn't mind. *I* didn't mind. It didn't feel wrong. I wasn't upset here. Josh, three months ago I could barely bring myself to even come into this room. I used to force myself to dust it but I couldn't look at the bed. But now I feel as if I'm me again, you see.'

He smiled as he took her hand. 'I'm glad. I'm glad, Paige. And relieved. That way at least I don't feel quite so guilty about taking advantage of you. And much as I'd like to celebrate by taking you back to bed again, I'm afraid I'll collapse unless you bring me food immediately.'

Paige frowned at him. 'You've never taken advantage of me, you silly man. It's the other way round.'

He turned her palm over and kissed it, the imprint of his mouth sending heat spiralling up her arm. 'You're wrong, but I'm too hungry to argue,' he declared deeply. 'I need food.'

'I'll do you Marmite on toast.' She slid her hand away

from him and pressed it to his cheek when his expression turned to dismay. 'Just as a snack. We're eating out tonight.' She ogled the towel he'd fastened around his bare waist and made a little mock tug at it. 'And if you really haven't the energy for sex, you'd better put some clothes on or I won't be able to restrain myself.'

'Bring me a sandwich and then you won't have to,' he growled, patting her bottom to send her out. 'I don't suppose you've got a beer in the house?'

'You're in Yorkshire,' she reminded him with a scathing look. 'Dad's left half that wardrobe there full of Tetley's.'

He smiled down at her. 'Paige, you are truly a dream woman.'

They had a wonderful meal in one of the village's Indian restaurants then she took him for a beer at her favourite pub. Their chatter was largely impersonal, but from time to time she caught him studying her quizzically. Later, in the privacy of the cottage, she brought him coffee and said bluntly, 'I was stupid to think I could stick to no sex, Josh. I can't be with you and not want you. Does that mean I'm a sex maniac?'

Taking a sip of the drink she'd passed him, he sent her an amused sideways look. 'I wish.'

'You'll change your mind in a few weeks when you get sick of me.' She was just going to have to accept that inevitably there was going to be heartache.

Josh sighed. 'Paige, I've told you I enjoy you being there.'

'Not when I flood the laundry—'

'Despite you flooding the laundry,' he corrected with a smile that was almost, although not quite, convincing enough to make her believe him. 'Despite you leaving your clothes all over the house. Despite even waking up covered in sweat because three fat blankets have mysteriously appeared on my bed.'

'I still have to find out about those duck feathers,' she declared, reminded abruptly of the main reason she preferred blankets to his duvets. 'I suspect—'

'Forget the ducks,' he said roughly. 'Paige, I'm saying I don't want you to go. I know I protest about things you do but that's partly a game we play. I don't mind so much.'

She worried her lower lip, thinking. 'There's still the issue of you wanting to get married and have children soon,' she ventured gingerly. 'No girlfriend's going to want me hanging about the house—'

'I'm not about to marry in a hurry simply to have children,' he said heavily. 'In the meantime, there's no reason you shouldn't have somewhere nice to live.'

'It might not be long before you find a wife,' she said quietly. 'Bunty's Catherine does sound pretty good—'

'I'll see her,' he said flatly, lifting up his hands in what looked like a gesture of surrender. 'She'll be at David's and Louise's next Saturday for dinner. Remember, she was Louise's chief bridesmaid, and you and Bunty aren't the only ones trying to set this up. I'll go if you will, too.'

'Me?' Paige recoiled. 'That'll look strange.'

'No one has to know we're together. I'll tell David you're in town and naturally he'll invite you along as well. I want you to be there.'

She shrugged a little helplessly. 'I suppose I could ask the cake man—'

'*No cake man.*' He looked exasperated. 'No cake man, Paige. We don't need more complications. You, me, Louise, David and this Catherine person. Deal?'

'I suppose I could make it back to London in time.' She looked around the room vaguely. 'There's not much more to do here. A couple of long days in the garden should finish things. I should be through by mid-week.'

'Make sure you are.' He finished his coffee then his

mouth curled into a smile. 'If you're not back by Friday night I'll come and fetch you.'

'Sometimes I can't imagine why I'm worried I might fall in love with you,' she declared when he took her tea away, even though she was barely halfway through it, and lifted her into his arms. 'You're extraordinarily bossy.'

'And stuffy.' He kissed her as he carried her towards the main bedroom. 'Demanding.'

'Very demanding.' She kept her arms around his neck when he lowered her to his bed so he had to come down with her.

'Of course, if you fall asleep on me again tonight before I've finished with you then I'm going to strangle you,' he said conversationally, as he stripped off her clothes. 'In which case this whole discussion has been purely academic.'

'I won't fall asleep,' she said huskily, wrapping her legs hard around his thighs. 'I am *definitely* staying awake for this.'

CHAPTER TEN

JOSH left on Sunday evening but he called Paige every night and they talked for hours, sometimes about what they'd been doing each day but mostly about nonsense and silly things so that she could never remember the conversations properly afterwards.

On Wednesday she piled up the Mini with her last load of things for the charity shops, and on Thursday morning she handed the keys to the agent who'd be looking after the house for her, called in at the cemetery to spend an hour talking to her parents, then set out for London.

Happily, the space outside Josh's home was large enough for three cars so she was able to squeeze in the Mini. Lights were on inside and Josh came out when she knocked. He returned her enthusiastic kiss warmly, then helped her unload her things.

'I couldn't wait to get here,' she declared, launching herself at him over her bags the minute he closed the front door behind them. 'Thank goodness you weren't late getting home from work. I've been chanting your name since the Northampton turn-off. I know this is probably very impolite but I want sex, please. Immediately.'

'Demanding floozy.' But he laughed as his hands slid beneath her jumper to cup her breasts. 'Get your gear off, then.'

She pulled her jumper over her head and then her T-shirt, quickly followed by her shoes, jeans and knickers. 'Socks on,' she decided out loud. 'Cold feet.'

'I refuse to make love to you when you're wearing non-matching socks.' Ignoring her laughing protests and evading her kicking feet easily, Josh tugged them off as he carried her upstairs over his shoulder fireman-style.

As soon as Josh left for work the next morning, Paige telephoned his ward to talk to Bunty. 'Come in for lunch today,' Bunty insisted, after greeting her news about Josh meeting Catherine on Saturday night enthusiastically. 'You can meet her and tell me what you think.'

Curious about having another look at the hospital where Josh spent so much of his time, Paige left the house early. She'd assumed Josh would be busy in his operating theatre but instead she spotted him immediately she walked onto Bunty's ward. He was half turned away from her, talking seriously to an older, worried-looking doctor in a white coat. 'So it's actually stuck?' she heard Josh say.

'The wire's hanging out of her mouth,' the other man said. 'I took the scope out but I can't move the basket. I've tried everything but it won't budge.'

Paige hesitated a few metres away, not wanting to interrupt, but she couldn't help but overhear their conversation.

'Have you ever heard of this happening before?' Josh was asking.

'Not here.' The other man shook his head. 'It's a first for me and I've been doing these for fifteen years now. I haven't a clue. She's not in any discomfort but I'd rather not leave her waiting too long. Josh, I'd really appreciate you taking a look.'

'If there's a theatre available I could take her now.' Josh checked his watch. 'Is she nil-by-mouth?'

'Nothing since six,' the older doctor confirmed. 'I've already checked with Theatres and any time before one-thirty is fine with them. I've explained everything to Mrs Harrison. Will you go in via a lap, or will it have to be open?'

'With luck all we'll need is a general anaesthetic,' Paige heard Josh say wryly. 'Once she's relaxed I might be able to pull the basket out without needing to cut. Leave it with me, Mike. Is she still in the endoscopy suite?'

'Ready and waiting,' the other man confirmed. Paige saw the older doctor looked a little embarrassed as he turned towards her. 'Thanks,' he said sheepishly. 'I'll come with you now if you'd like to meet her. And I'd like to come to Theatre to watch if you don't mind.'

'Fine.' Josh was nodding. 'Of course.' He turned as if to go with the other man, then stopped when he saw Paige. 'Mike, I'll catch you up,' he called. 'Paige…?' He took a step towards her. 'What are you doing here?'

'I'm meeting Bunty,' Paige explained quickly. 'We're having lunch. That sounded interesting. What's happened? What's stuck?'

'Mike was doing an ERCP,' he said absently. 'That means putting a tube down someone's throat and through the stomach to get access to the bile ducts. He was trying to get gallstones out of the duct, but the Dormia basket got stuck and he can't pull it out. Paige, I'm not sure I like the thought of you and Bunty—'

'It doesn't matter what you like,' she said lightly. 'How can anyone possibly leave a basket inside somebody?'

'It's very small.'

'What are you going to do?'

'Get it out,' he said with exaggerated patience. 'I'm going to get it out. Paige—'

'Oh, here's Bunty.' Paige beamed as the nurse bustled up. 'I'm all ready,' she told her. 'Josh has to go and take a basket out of some poor lady's tummy.'

'Do you, Josh?' Paige saw that Bunty looked as surprised as she'd been by that. 'Whose tummy?'

'Take some stickies,' Josh said sharply, passing her what Paige saw was a sheet of printed labels, presumably bearing the details of the lady with the basket. 'She's a medical patient but she'll need to come into one of your beds after Theatre. What are you up to, Bunty?'

'I've already explained,' Paige pointed out. 'Bunty and I are having lunch.'

'I'll just organise this bed first,' said Bunty, and she bustled away with the labels.

Paige smiled at Josh. 'You're very sexy when you're at work,' she whispered. 'I was feeling quite flushed just listening to you. Do you think you might be home early tonight?'

'I'll call you.' The half-frustrated narrowing of his dark eyes suggested he was still struggling to come to terms with the thought of her and Bunty spending time together. 'In the meantime, be good.'

Paige arched her brows at him as he walked around her to leave. 'Of course, Josh.'

'Catherine's waiting for us on the second level,' Bunty said as she came hurrying back a minute or two later. 'Paige, I really think this is going to work. Josh has been so cheerful I think he must be looking forward to Saturday night.'

'He could be, I suppose,' Paige said doubtfully, although she suspected Bunty might be getting hopeful prematurely. Josh had mentioned Saturday's dinner again the night before, reminding her she'd agreed to go along as well, but he seemed to be going into the almost-blind date with more sufferance than enthusiasm.

Catherine was beautiful—tall and slender with sweet, even features and lovely big blue eyes, she had shiny blonde hair cut into a perfect bob and she was the neatest eater Paige had ever seen. While they chatted, Catherine cut her apple muffin into twelve, and her appetite was clearly delicate because, with all the care she'd taken to slice the muffin symmetrically, she ate less than half of it before making a little moue and putting it away with the air of someone whose stomach was well and truly satisfied.

Paige, who'd shoved her own whole double chocolate muffin thoughtlessly right up to her mouth and devoured it, was sure she must have chocolate and crumbs from one side of her face to the other, yet she still felt hungry. She also felt like a piggy lump.

'So, Catherine...' she wiped a paper napkin across her mouth as surreptitiously as she could manage after she'd swallowed the last of her cake '...are you nervous about Saturday?'

'Oh, no.' The other woman was busy with a compact mirror and a lip brush, reapplying what looked to Paige like still-immaculate lipstick. 'Not nervous at all. I've known for ages how suited Josh and I are.' She exchanged smiles with Bunty. 'Bunty and I thought the wedding would be when he'd make a move, but he left...' Catherine blinked at her '...unexpectedly early.'

Paige felt guilty. 'I should warn you that he's a bit of an order freak,' she said delicately. 'To the extent of being stuffy. His home's like a museum and he notices if one little thing is out of place.'

'Me, too.' The other woman folded her compact shut with a snap, her smile pleased. 'I can't bear disorder.'

'He's extremely punctual,' Bunty added.

Catherine nodded. 'I pride myself on my punctuality.'

'He wants children.' Paige exchanged a quick glance with a beaming Bunty, then looked back at Catherine, watching her carefully. 'Not just one, but lots. Soon.'

'He's perfect,' Catherine trilled smoothly. 'I adore children.'

'He hates shopping.'

'All men do,' Catherine declared. 'They're happier left at home.'

'How do you feel about blankets?'

'Blankets?'

'Do you like blankets on your bed?'

'I prefer a duvet.' The other woman was frowning slightly now. 'Blankets are so messy. Duvets filled with duck down are the best. They're warm as well as tidy. Why? Does Josh have allergies?'

'None that I'm aware of,' Paige said briefly. She looked at Bunty, who was still beaming triumphantly, and back at Catherine, then lifted her hands in the air. 'Bunty's right,' she declared. 'Speaking as someone who's known Josh for years, Catherine, I think you're perfect for each other. I think Saturday night is going to go very well.'

'I know.' Catherine smiled. 'I can't wait.'

'Neither can I.' But Paige's smile felt stiff so she tried it again more firmly this time. 'Neither can I, Catherine.'

'So you're *absolutely* sure David and Louise don't mind me tagging along tonight?' Paige repeated, watching Josh's face carefully as she dressed on Saturday evening.

'For the eleventh and final time, they are delighted,' Josh said evenly. 'Paige, is it really that hard to face seeing them together?'

'For the hundredth and final time, it isn't that,' she retorted. She unfastened the packet containing the stockings she'd bought and sat on the edge of the bed to make them easier to pull on. 'I don't have a problem facing Louise. Or David. I don't know why you're being so pig-headed about him. I truly am happy for them. It's just I still feel as if I'm imposing—'

'You're not,' he said heavily, 'imposing.'

'What if Louise minds—?'

'She won't.' She looked up to see him watching her intently. He still had his towel around him from after his shower, she noted, and he hadn't even begun to get dressed. 'What are you doing?'

'Putting on my stockings.' She lifted one leg straight off the bed and tugged the sheer fabric smoothly up to her thighs, where she fastened it in three places to her new suspender belt. 'I read about them in a magazine at the hospital yesterday. They're supposed to be much better for you than tights.'

'I've never seen you wearing them before.'

'That's because I've just bought them.' She pulled the other stocking on then stood to fasten it, bending over slightly to adjust the length. Her hands on her hips, she inspected herself in Josh's mirror, twirling a little one way then the other and arching her back to see how they looked. 'Do you think I should have put my knickers on first or am I supposed to wear them over the top?'

'I think that we're going to be late for dinner.' With a suddenness that took her completely by surprise, he shed his towel then came for her, lifting her feet right off the floor and dumping her onto the bed.

'There's no time,' she squealed, laughing against his shower-damp shoulder as he followed her urgently down. 'Josh...no! We can't.'

'David knows I'm bringing you.' He covered her mouth with an urgency that made her grateful she hadn't got around to putting any make-up on yet. 'He'll know who to blame when we're late.'

'What about Catherine?' she protested vaguely, curling up, opening her mouth against his shoulder as he moved down her body.

His mouth lingered at her stomach. 'Later.'

They weren't terribly late. 'Only a little over half an hour,' she declared, leaning over to inspect the illuminated clock on Josh's dashboard as he reversed into a slot outside what he'd told her was David's new home in Chiswick. 'That's polite in some circles.'

David looked good, Paige thought in the brief pause between him coming to the door and letting them in. He'd gained weight, but it suited him, and he looked radiantly happy. 'Paige!' he cried, lunging at her when she came up the steps. 'You look delicious,' he declared, after pressing a rather startling kiss on her mouth. 'Gorgeous. As always. We were thrilled when we heard you were in town. I can't believe it's been so long. You haven't aged a week. Come in. Hi, Josh.'

Paige dimly heard Josh saying something in the background, but her attention was on the hesitant-looking, dark-haired woman who was waiting for them inside. Paige thought she looked about the same age as she was, and she thought she was very pretty.

'Louise, meet Paige, the other love of my life,' David was saying cheerfully, his arm still around Paige's shoulders as he drew her further inside. 'Paige, this is my wife, Louise.'

Paige felt Josh's level regard prickling at the side of her face, but although she still didn't understand why he still doubted her feelings for David she didn't let him distract her.

'Hello, Louise.' She shook the other woman's hand warmly. 'Take no notice of your husband. I was never one of the loves of his life. He's pretending to forget but, truly, after about three weeks I drove him crazy. I'm so pleased to meet you at last. Josh has told me all about you and, well, I'm just thrilled David's been lucky enough to find someone so lovely.'

The other woman visibly relaxed at that and Paige knew for sure then that Josh had overestimated her confidence. A woman would have to be almost arrogantly sure of herself, Paige thought, to carry off meeting a husband's former girlfriend without any reaction at all, and she was pleased for David's sake that Louise didn't take him quite that much for granted.

'Please, come in, Paige.' The other woman's smile had turned warm now. 'Hasn't it been cool today? Just when we thought we were going to have a proper summer, it's changed again. David, take Paige's coat. The heating's on in the other rooms, Paige, so you won't need it. Come and see Catherine. She's looking forward to seeing you again. She was telling us she met you yesterday.'

Out of the corner of her eye Paige saw Josh's dark gaze narrow at that, but she avoided his eye and kept well away from him.

'Josh, you remember Catherine, don't you?' Louise looked excited as she showed them into the living room. 'My chief bridesmaid.'

'Of course.' Paige thought that Josh handled the introduction very smoothly. With a casual nod of his head and a smile, he came forward and took her hand then kissed her cheek. 'Hello, Catherine. How have you been?'

'Josh.' Catherine sounded breathless, Paige thought. 'Fine. How nice to see you again.'

They exchanged a few general remarks while Paige admired the house to Louise, then David interrupted them all by clapping his hands.

'Right,' he said heartily. 'Beer for you, Josh, I presume.' He held up a couple of bottles. 'Paige, what about you? Louise has bought stuff for pina coladas.'

Paige blinked. 'A pina colada would be…incredible,' she said slowly, bemused that he'd remembered her liking for the cocktail. She followed David's pleased-looking wife out into the kitchen. 'Once I drank these like water,' she confided. 'When I was studying they were my special treat to myself. But I haven't had one in years.'

'David said you liked them.' Louise had the blender set up. She passed Paige a carton of pineapple juice to open while she busied herself with a tin of coconut cream. 'He said you used to come home on Friday nights and mix up a big batch, only half the time you'd forget to put the lid on the blender and the whole sticky mess would fly out all over his walls.'

Paige laughed. 'Don't believe all his stories,' she warned. 'That only happened a couple of times. I expect David's been trying to make me sound like a monster.'

'He has a bit.' But Louise smiled back. 'Probably trying to make sure I don't get jealous. But I told him I didn't believe him. I told him you couldn't possibly be as bad as he said because he let you stay two years.'

Paige hesitated. 'Louise, you do know that, despite all that time, we were only a couple for a few weeks in the very beginning?'

'Yes, he told me.' Louise smiled again as she loosened the top of a bottle of rum. 'He said you ended it but in the end he agreed with you. He said you were completely incompatible.'

'True.' Paige blinked as she saw how much alcohol Louise added, although her trepidation abated a little when the rum was followed by loads of ice. 'I'm glad he explained that. I'd like us to be friends.'

'I'd like that, too.' Louise put the lid on the blender and screwed the middle bit tight. 'How long are you in London and where are you staying? You know, we have a spare room here if you need somewhere to crash.'

Fortunately, the noise of the blender then the excitement of pouring their drinks and tasting the mixture distracted Louise from expecting any reply to her questions. Paige didn't want to mislead her intentionally, but Catherine and Louise were obviously close and she didn't want to risk Catherine being concerned by the thought of her temporarily living with Josh.

'Wonderful,' Paige declared, after a mouthful of the cocktail. Stronger than she was used to, the drink nevertheless had the sweet, sickly coconut flavour she remembered and loved.

David and Josh stuck with beer and Catherine preferred white wine, so that Paige and Louise were left to demolish the entire blender of pina colada alone. Then Louise murmured something about needing to make a sauce, and when she waved aside Paige's offer of help David offered to show her their home.

'Leave them to it,' he suggested, gesturing towards where Josh and Catherine were talking hospital talk. 'I want to get you alone.'

Josh must have had at least half an ear on their conversation because he looked up sharply at that, his eyes narrowing on Paige's face. Paige rolled her eyes at him, before following David out the far door.

'The main dining area,' he told her, showing her into a large room where the table was already set and French doors opened out onto a courtyard with plants in terracotta pots. 'Downstairs powder room, my study,' he continued, opening doors.

'You used to tell me GPs didn't make any money,' she reminded him, following him up a narrow flight of stairs. 'That must have been an outrageous lie.'

'Between us we make enough to support a mortgage,' he said lightly. 'We won't own it much before we retire. Like it?'

'It's great.' She looked around the top part's three bedrooms and two bathrooms. 'When did you move?'

'A few weeks before the wedding.'

'Did you know with Louise very quickly?'

'Not as quickly as with you.'

'But you didn't love me.'

'For a long time I was sure I did.'

'But now you know how the real thing feels so you've forgotten all about me.'

'I still think you're gorgeous.' He grinned back at her. 'Quite scrumptiously gorgeous. If I hadn't found myself the most wonderful wife in the world you might have had to fight me off again. So, what's going on, Paige? What are you doing to poor Josh?'

'Josh isn't poor.'

'Neatly sidestepping the question.'

He'd sat on the edge of the bed in what Paige assumed was a guest bedroom and was now eyeing her speculatively, so she turned away from him deliberately and went to the window and looked down into the street. 'If you ask silly questions, people will sidestep them.'

'Come off it, Paige. You used to fancy him rotten.'

She whirled around, her eyes wide. 'Why on earth would you say that?'

'I know you.' He tilted his head, his brown eyes dancing at her. 'That night he brought that Melinda to supper you were ready to rip her eyes out.'

'Because she was awful—'

'Because she was getting into Josh. You were green.'

'You're confusing my emotions with your own,' she countered immediately. 'You were the jealous one that night. You were jealous of Josh. Your eyes just about popped out of your head when Melinda walked in.'

'She was,' he responded, laughing now, 'very sexy. You hadn't slept with me in almost a year. I was easily excited in those days.'

'Well, you missed your chance.' Paige rolled her eyes. 'Josh told me that nothing happened with her. They were just colleagues. You should have made a move, David.'

'You wish.' He was still laughing. 'Leaving Josh alone for you to comfort, I suppose. That's what you really wanted. Just once, admit it.' When she clamped her lips together he threw a pillow at her. 'Come on, Paige,' he taunted. 'Spill the beans. I saw the way he was looking at you downstairs. You two have to be sleeping together.'

'You haven't changed one bit.' She threw the pillow back at him. 'You're still obsessed with Josh's sex life.'

'Ah, but I have changed,' he said easily, tossing the pillow back to her again. 'Even two years ago, just thinking about you and Josh together would have given me a stroke. Now it just makes me worry for the poor bloke.'

'For the last time, he's not poor.' Gritting her teeth, Paige came at him with the pillow, intent on smothering his teasing laughter. 'You're a nosy man, David Leigh.' She pushed him back and pretended to press down on the pillow, squealing as he threw mock punches at her until finally, still laughing, she subsided onto the bed beside him.

'Why didn't you come to our wedding?'

She groaned. 'I was late. I got there as you were leaving. That's how I met Josh again. I hadn't organised anywhere to stay so he kindly took me home to his place.'

'*Kind*, was he?' David lifted his head, his eyes dancing. 'That's an interesting way of looking at it. Does Catherine know you're living with Josh?'

'*Staying* with him,' Paige insisted. 'You're so boring.' She sat up and slapped his rounded stomach. 'Come on. We should go. And, remember, we shared a house, quite innocently, for years.'

'But I'm a wimp,' he said, levering himself off the bed. 'Josh isn't. Hasn't he taught you that yet?'

Louise was busy in the kitchen when they came downstairs and David went in to see her. Seeing that the other woman was looking a little flustered over the sauce she was whisking, Paige retreated and returned to the other room.

Meeting Josh's hard look with a deliberately bland smile, she took the couch opposite him and Catherine then leaned forward and helped herself to a big handful of crisps. 'Upstairs is lovely,' she said finally, when it appeared that her arrival had brought an end to their intellectual-sounding conversation about some poor little boy with leukaemia on Catherine's ward. 'They've done a lovely job. David did the papering and painting himself, you know.'

Conscious of their audience, Josh regarded Paige steadily, although inwardly he was furious. He didn't know who he was more angry with. Paige, for the giggles he'd heard from upstairs and for her flushed cheeks and disordered hair. Or David, who he felt like hauling out of the kitchen and beating slowly and satisfyingly to a bloody pulp. Wanting to be violent wasn't a sensation he was used to, but he felt it now. 'You've been studying walls, then?' he enquired, barely concealing his disbelief.

'Intently.' Paige gritted her teeth at him, wondering what she'd done now to make Josh look so grumpy. 'David's always had a knack for home improvements.'

'You obviously have an interest in them yourself,' he observed, 'for you to have spent so much time discussing them.'

'I was fascinated.' She stared back as hard as he was staring at her.

'More drinks, anyone?' David, looking flushed, poked his head through into the room. He looked relieved when they all shook their heads. 'Bit of a delay on the sauce front,' he mouthed, rolling his eyes at them before disappearing back into the kitchen.

'Josh has a lovely home, Catherine.' Paige directed her smile to the other woman. 'But it needs a lot of work to bring it up to date.'

'I'm very good with interior decorating,' Catherine said pleasantly. 'It's the sort of challenge I enjoy.' She smiled at Josh. 'I'd be happy to give you some suggestions.'

'Thank you, Catherine.' But his smile had a hint of steel when he included Paige in it. 'That's very kind.'

'Catherine was telling me she adores children,' Paige

said pointedly. 'How many would you like, Catherine? Three?'

'Or more.' Catherine looked pleased. 'I think my love of children's the reason I find my work so rewarding. Do you, Josh?'

'Find my work rewarding?' he drawled. 'Yes, I suppose I do.'

Paige knew exactly what he was doing but she saw that Catherine looked confused. Speaking quickly so the other woman wouldn't be embarrassed, Paige said, 'We were talking about bedding yesterday, Josh. Catherine was saying how much she likes duvets. Down duvets. Down from ducks. I was thinking what a coincidence that was.'

'Oh.' Josh quirked an eyebrow. 'Why do you say that, Paige?'

'Because—' She stopped, frowning as she realised she could hardly admit to an intimate knowledge of his bedding preferences. 'Oh, well, because... What do you prefer?'

'Lately, blankets,' he said coolly, his eyes narrowing on hers.

Paige wasn't used to the sensation of blushing, but the abrupt burning sensation on her cheeks told her that she just might be doing that. 'But blankets are so untidy.'

'That's what I think.' Catherine had been looking confused again but now she looked relieved to have something to contribute. 'And they fall off during the night and they have to be tucked in all the time. Duvets are so much more functional.'

'But are they warm enough?' Josh said mildly. 'And what about the down? Have you ever thought where that comes from, Catherine? Have you ever thought about the ducks from which the down or even the feathers come? Have you ever wondered if perhaps some of them might have been sacrificed to supply down for your duvets?'

While Paige pulled rude faces at him, Catherine regarded

him a little doubtfully. 'I've never thought about it at all,' the other woman protested. 'Why would I? Even if they do sacrifice them, they're only birds. There are far more important things to worry about in the world than a few creatures with feathers, aren't there, Josh? Things like wars and child abuse and prisoners of conscience. I mean, it's not as if it's worth working ourselves up into a state about something as trivial as the welfare of birds.'

'I still sometimes wonder.'

Josh's pensive look made Paige want to thump him. 'Catherine was saying she's a very tidy person,' she said loudly. 'She can't abide mess. I was telling her you're exactly the same.'

'I'm not as tidy as I used to be,' he retorted calmly. 'I've been finding discarded clothes all around the place lately. Perhaps I'm changing my habits.'

'I don't think men enjoy shopping,' Catherine said baldly. 'If I were married I'd never expect my husband to come to the supermarket.'

She sent Josh what looked to Paige to be a rather challenging look, but to Paige's fury Josh put on a surprised face. 'I don't mind supermarkets,' he said, the blatant lie just about making Paige gasp out loud. 'In fact, with the right companion, shopping can be very entertaining.'

Paige winced at the wounded look Catherine directed her way. 'But you don't actually like it,' Paige said almost pleadingly. 'I mean, if you were married you'd be happy if your wife volunteered to do it for you, wouldn't you, Josh?'

He smiled at her. 'I like to think I'd want to spend every free moment I had with my wife, Paige. If that meant sharing supermarket chores then, of course, I'd want to do that.'

The door to the kitchen opened and Paige sent David a desperate look. 'Everything's ready in the other room,' he told them. 'Go through. Louise is lighting the candles.'

'Oh, this looks beautiful, Louise.' Paige touched David's wife's arm as they walked in. 'And everything smells delicious.'

Louise's smile was definitely uneven. 'You're our first dinner party,' she said shakily. 'I've been a bit nervous.'

'Not to mention very dizzy.' David's arm curved around his wife's waist. 'Half a bucket of pina colada's a bit more than you're used to, sweetheart. You shouldn't have tried to keep up with Paige. She can drink like a fish.'

'Only pina coladas.' Paige smiled apologetically. 'Anything else sends me silly. Where shall we sit, Louise?'

'Oh, Josh there, Catherine there, you there, Paige.' Louise waved her hand vaguely in different directions. 'I'll get the rest of the food.'

Paige knew she was meant to be beside Louise, leaving Catherine and Josh together on the opposite side of the table, but before she could move that way Josh unexpectedly pushed her down into the seat beside him. She saw Catherine's puzzled look and poked him in the ribs and under cover of the conversation hissed something rude, but he ignored her.

'It's watercress,' Louise said, referring to the soup as she passed it around once everyone was seated. 'Everything's vegetarian, Paige. David said you never used to eat meat and as we weren't sure if you'd changed...'

'How lovely. Thank you.' Paige was touched her hostess had gone to so much trouble. 'I am still mostly but I would have just eaten the vegetables if you'd done meat. But...' She faltered as Josh's hand curled around her thigh beneath the table. 'But thank you.'

Unable to slap his hand away because she was taking her soup, she jerked her leg, but he merely sent her a cool look and continued inching up her skirt until it gathered at her hips, leaving her—apart from her stockings—virtually naked beneath the table.

CHAPTER ELEVEN

HAVING to take his own soup forced Josh's hand away, but it came back when he started eating, his left hand fondling the strip of bare thigh above Paige's stockings while he joined in with the dinner conversation, his voice completely steady and unemotional.

Paige, in the meantime, had gone dizzy. As unobtrusively as she could, she kept putting her hand down and trying to force his away, but against him her strength was puny and she couldn't budge him. Without taking the risk of embarrassing their hosts and Catherine, she realised there was nothing she could do but be grateful his caress wasn't turning more intimate.

'Paige...?' She looked up, blinking, at Josh's soft voice, realising that everyone was looking at her as if it wasn't the first time he'd spoken to her. 'What do you think?' he said interestedly.

'Me?' Paige blinked again, still finding it difficult to concentrate with his hand fondling her quite so deliberately.

'About Tiger,' he said softly. 'I was telling David we'd been down to see Tiger.'

'Tiger's great.' Paige looked at David. 'Mmm. You missed a great dog there.'

'My loss.' But David laughed. 'You should have seen this thing, Louise. He was the ugliest mongrel ever born. Paige cried for hours when I wouldn't let her have him in the house, but poor Josh wasn't strong enough to stand up to that treatment.'

'Obviously Josh is a true gentleman,' Catherine said with a smile.

At that moment Paige could have told her precisely why Josh wasn't a gentleman at all, but she refrained. 'I've been meaning to ask you, Josh,' she blurted instead. 'Whatever happened to the lady with the basket in her tummy the other day?'

'Basket in her tummy?' David, like Louise and Catherine, looked startled. 'What was that, Josh?'

'One of the physicians had a problem with a Dormia basket getting stuck during ERCP,' Josh said fluidly, and the nods of the other three suggested that, unlike Paige, they all understood what he was saying. 'We thought I was going to have to operate to get it out but, happily, once we had our patient relaxed under general anaesthetic the basket came out easily through her mouth.'

'Does that mean you didn't have to operate?' Paige asked quickly, hoping a barrage of questions might distract him from her thighs. 'Is she all right now? Was the basket all right? Does this sort of thing happen all the time?'

'Yes. Yes, she's fine. She went home the next day. No. No.' Irritatingly, his bland smile and the teasing movements of his fingers suggested he'd seen through her ploy.

After the main course and dessert they returned to the other room for coffee, and Paige made sure she sat as far away from him as she could. As they were finishing she saw Louise beginning to suppress yawns so she sent Josh a pointed look then turned to her hosts and said, 'It's late. Thank you for a lovely dinner but I should be calling a cab.'

She'd warned Josh in advance that she'd be getting a cab home, to leave him free to drive Catherine, but to her fury he stood. 'You're right, Paige. It is late. Catherine, can we give you a lift?'

'Thank you, Josh.' Catherine sent Paige a vaguely confused look and Paige gritted her teeth again.

'I'm taking a cab,' she said firmly to Josh.

'Nonsense.'

'I insist.'

'You're being ridiculous.'

She met his quiet regard fiercely, relieved that Catherine and Louise and David now seemed preoccupied with their farewells and fetching coats and weren't taking any notice of their conversation. 'Stop it.'

He looked impatient. 'Paige—'

'Stop ruining everything,' she whispered, glancing behind her to check that the others were still busy. 'If you don't take her home I'll never talk to you again.'

His face went abruptly cold. 'All right.' He barely looked at her. 'If it's that important to you. Remembered your keys?'

'In my coat,' she confirmed quietly. 'I'll be fine.'

'What about money?'

'Oh.' She caught her lower lip between her teeth. 'I forgot. Lend me ten pounds?'

'Take twenty.' He took a note out of his wallet. 'I don't want this, Paige.'

'I'm thinking of you,' she whispered. 'Stop fighting me on this, Josh. Please. Trust me. It's for the best.'

Only standing with David and Louise by the gate, waiting for her cab to arrive, while she waved at Josh as he drove away with a laughing and obviously delighted Catherine, it suddenly didn't feel like it was for the best for Paige.

Her cab wasn't long in coming and the trip back to Josh's house was relatively efficient. She spent the first part of the night sitting on the stairs wrapped in her blankets, thinking, and the second part of the night sitting on the stairs wrapped in more blankets, waiting for Josh.

But when the sun came up Paige finally had to acknowledge that he wouldn't be coming home to her. She started to cry. When that stopped she was tired to her bones, but she couldn't have slept so she dragged her stiff body up to her bathroom and ran herself a bath.

Knowing that she'd brought everything on herself, it didn't make her feel any less wretched.

She washed her hair and soaked in the warm water until her muscles felt marginally more mobile. When she got out she dried and cleaned the bath then dressed and went to make herself tea.

The digital display on Josh's microwave told her that it was eleven-thirty, and when she heard the key in the outside door it read eleven fifty-six. 'Paige, I'm sorry.' She heard his steps on the stairs and then he was checking his watch as he came towards her. 'Sorry I'm late.'

He was still wearing his suit from the night before, of course, but its immaculate appearance suggested that whatever his haste to make love to Catherine, one of them at least had taken the time to hang up his clothes. 'I had to go into work for a round before I came home and there were a few things to sort out. Had you made plans? I didn't think to ask last night. Was there anything in particular you wanted to do today?'

'Nothing firm.' She jerked her cheek away when he bent to kiss her, and went to the sink, pretending a need to wash her cup. 'What about Catherine?'

'What about Catherine?'

She wiped out the cup very carefully. 'Aren't you seeing her today?'

'I hadn't arranged to.'

'Just tonight, then?'

'No.'

Paige swung around. 'Then don't you think you should be?' she demanded.

He frowned. 'Paige—'

'Josh, how do you think she feels?' she cried, feeling the

pain herself. 'Catherine's not the sort of woman to go in for one-night stands.'

'I didn't say she was—'

'You should be with her now.'

'I thought we were going to do something today.'

'But you can't. Not after last night. You can't leave her. You might lose her, Josh, if you treat her like this.'

'I won't—'

'You must know how perfect she is.'

'Yes.' His suddenly calm agreement took her breath away. 'You're right. She is. Perfect.'

'I'm…right?' Paige sagged against the cupboards. 'You mean you believe that now?'

'Catherine's everything you said she'd be. She's intelligent, knowledgeable and an excellent nurse. She loves children so I expect she'll be a superb mother. She's neat—her flat's amazingly clean by the way—and orderly. She's just perfect.'

'I told you so.' But she spoke the words automatically because her head was spinning. 'What's going to happen now?'

'Now I'm going to get out of these clothes and take a shower. Want to join me?'

Paige recoiled, genuinely shocked. 'Of course not,' she gasped.

'Up to you.' He lifted one shoulder casually as he turned away. 'If you want, we could go to Pimlico this afternoon. I hear that new exhibition's good.'

'I don't think so, Josh.' But she was speaking to the door because he'd already gone, so she just stayed there, numb, listening to his steps on the stairs.

Minutes later her temper flared. She tore up the stairs, two at a time. 'By the way,' she shouted from the door of his bathroom, keeping her eyes averted from the glass shower cubicle, 'that hand-under-the-table trick last night was particularly disgustingly outrageous. Pervert!'

'Hey!' His laughing protest stopped her before she could get out of the room and brought her back, fuming. 'How did you expect me to react?' he shouted. 'All I could think about all evening was you in those stockings. If you're going to wear those things you have to expect that.'

'Me in those stockings is obviously not all you thought about last night,' she shrieked.

'How do you know?'

'If it was, you'd have come home.'

The water shut off abruptly and he hauled back the glass door. 'Jealous?'

She threw a towel in his direction. 'Why would I be?'

'You tell me.' He'd caught the towel and to her relief wrapped it around his hips. 'Hmm? Isn't everything going exactly the way you planned it?'

'I didn't expect you to jump into bed with her last night.'

'You sent me home with her.'

'I didn't think you were going to spend the night,' she cried.

'So when was I supposed to do that?'

'I thought you'd get to know her first.'

'You didn't think we got to know each other at dinner?'

'Not well enough to have sex.'

He balanced his hip against the door, his expression amused. 'So how long did you expect me to spend with the woman you want me to marry before we made love?'

'A few dates,' she said huskily.

'Two? Three?'

'Six or so.' She traced the pattern of his carpet with her bare foot. 'Perhaps a few more.'

'A few more?'

'I just think you're treating this too casually.'

'You're jealous as hell,' he said softly.

'I am a…little bit jealous,' she conceded. 'I didn't expect to be but, yes, I am.'

'Why? You wanted me to go out with her.'

'I *thought* I wanted that.'

'What's changed your mind?'

'I told you. I was jealous. Watching you drive her away last night made me feel…a bit sick. I wasn't expecting that.' She flexed her toes. 'I know that you meeting Catherine's the best thing that could have happened to you, but I didn't expect to…mind that much when you liked her. I didn't think I'd be so selfish. I knew I wouldn't like it that much but I thought I'd be happy for you.'

'Paige, how do you think I felt when you came downstairs with David last night?'

Her head jerked up. 'Why would you feel anything?'

'We'd heard you laughing. He was flushed. You were pink and your hair was all over the place. You looked like a woman who'd been thoroughly kissed. How do you think that made me feel?'

'We hadn't been kissing—we had a pillow fight. He was being silly and I tried to make him shut up with the pillow. Josh, David is devoted to Louise. We were just fooling around.'

He'd folded his arms and was watching her steadily. 'So why were you so against the idea of giving them that fertility doll you bought?'

'There was a reason but I really can't talk about it,' she said slowly. 'It's none of my business.'

'Is it because David was worried about his fertility?'

'You know that?'

'I remember when he had mumps,' he said smoothly. 'He had some doubts but he had a test before the wedding which showed he shouldn't have any problems.'

'He would never get himself tested,' Paige burst out, relieved that David had had good news. 'I could never understand why not when he used to worry so much about it. He was a GP, for goodness' sake, but he seemed to want to stay ignorant. I couldn't understand why he wouldn't just face up to it and get it over with.'

'Is that why it didn't work out between you two?'

'Of course not.' The absurdity of that made her laugh. 'David's fertility or lack of it didn't make a scrap of difference to me. If I'd been in love with him and we'd married, we could have adopted or done…whatever it is people do in these circumstances. But you must see why I thought that giving him the doll might seem a little insensitive.'

'At the time I thought your reluctance was a symptom of you still being in love with him.'

'Oh, for heaven's sake!' She kicked the wall. 'How many times do I have to tell you that that's ridiculous? You're determined not to believe me, aren't you, Josh? The truth is, I'm thrilled—*thrilled*—he's found Louise.'

'Then why don't you want me?'

Paige froze. 'I wasn't aware that I'd been offered you,' she said finally, stiffly. 'I wasn't aware that you were available to me.'

'We were stupid three years ago,' he said impatiently. 'Don't,' he ordered, lifting his hand to stop her when she started to protest. 'Stop pretending, Paige. You know exactly what I mean. We shouldn't have been so bloody noble. And you should have told me you weren't lovers. He'd have got over it eventually.'

'This is silly.' Her legs were weak and shaky. She went to his bed and sat on the edge of it. 'It's old history. I couldn't have told you. I couldn't have done it to him and you know you couldn't have either. Not then. Besides, you've met someone special now.'

'I met someone special the day David brought you into that pub to meet me,' he said calmly. 'Those times with David and you, those weekends away, that time we were stuck on that lake in the thunderstorm, that night with Melinda, that incredible day in the café, I was in love with you.'

Paige fell back on the bed, her heart pounding. She squeezed her eyes shut. 'Even if something had happened after that day in the café, six months later it would all have been over,' she said raggedly. 'I still would have wanted to look after Dad. It's just that it might have killed me to leave you. Instead, I didn't mind too much about leaving London. Everything worked out for the best.'

'Like hell it did.' She felt the dip as he sat on the bed, then his hand brushing her hair back from her forehead. 'I'd have come with you. I would have had to work out my notice but I could have found work in Yorkshire.'

'You'd have done that?' Her eyes flew open. 'For me?'

'Of course.' His eyes smiled down at her. 'Silly woman. It wasn't just a case of wanting to get into your knickers, Paige.' His hand probed under her skirt. 'Although the thought gave me more than a few sleepless nights. I loved you. In those days if I'd thought there'd been a chance of you loving me in return I'd have given you the world.'

'I was confused about my feelings,' she said thickly. She still thought they'd done the right thing by not hurting David, but her heart was heavy with the thought of what might have been. 'You could have come to Malton to visit me.'

'How was I to know you wanted that? I thought you loved David. How was I to know that whatever attraction you'd felt towards me hadn't been fleeting?'

'So you forgot about me.'

'Not *forgot* exactly.' Josh shrugged one shoulder. 'Men are pragmatic creatures, Paige.'

'*Fickle*, you mean.' She came up onto her elbows. 'And you did forget. There certainly wasn't any love in the way you looked at me when I arrived at the wedding. You looked fed up.'

'You'd almost run over my foot.'

'I missed it by metres.' Abruptly remembering where else his probing hands had been, she slapped them away and crossed her legs. 'So, was she good?'

'Who?'

'Catherine.'

'Mmm. More friendly than you.'

He slid his hand up from the waistband of her skirt to cup one breast, and when she felt her nipple crest beneath his caress she made a disgusted sound and jackknifed off the bed.

'When's the wedding?'

He rolled over onto his back, his expression lazy. 'Any thoughts?'

'None.' She was shaken by his matter-of-factness.

'I don't want anything big. Three or four weeks sounds about right.'

Paige paled. 'That's fast work.'

'I've taken things too slowly in the past.' He looked thoughtful. 'I've been too careful and too conservative. Now I'm going to go for what I want.'

'I'll go flat-hunting,' she declared thickly. 'Catherine won't want me here now you're engaged.'

'No hurry, Paige.' He smiled. 'Catherine understands. I thought it only fair to tell her.'

'Terrific.' She gritted her teeth at him. 'I'm so happy for you both.'

Josh watched Paige stomp away then lay back on the bed and smiled at the sounds of her slamming things about downstairs. But the defiant sound of the washing-machine door being closed brought him up fast. Teasing her a little had seemed appropriate punishment for her refusal to ac-knowledge her feelings for him, but he wasn't prepared to take a risk on his floor giving way beneath more flood-waters.

He bounded downstairs in his bare feet, registering her pink face and furious expression with satisfaction. 'I heard the washing machine.'

'Yes, you did.' She glared at him. 'Calm down. It won't overflow. I'm going to sit here and watch the bloody thing.'

Josh clicked his tongue at the swear word, earning himself a savage look. 'Why not admit it, Paige?'

'Admit what?'

'That you love me,' he said pleasantly.

'Why don't you admit you're an arrogant pig with the morals of an alley cat?' she retorted swiftly.

He laughed. 'I didn't spend the night with her, nasty woman. I went back to David's. I needed to talk to him. We drank till after four and since I couldn't have driven I stayed. I'm not interested in Catherine.'

'But she's perfect.'

'She does seem to be,' he conceded. 'But, much as I admire her thoughts on some things…' he smiled, knowing that would irritate her '…we'd bore one another silly. I was bored last night before you forced me to take her home. I've taken some time to be sure of myself this time, Paige, but I know exactly what I want now. I want you. Permanently.'

Stunned big eyes blinked up at him. 'You want me to be the mother of your children?'

'When you're ready.' He lifted one shoulder dismissively. 'If we're to be so blessed. But I want you more, Paige. Having the right wife, the right mother, is far more important than the timing of when our children are born.'

'I do love you, Josh.'

'Of course you do.' He laughed at her affronted expression and bent to kiss her forehead. 'I knew for sure last night. You wore those stockings deliberately to sabotage last night, Paige. Those stockings were your way of keeping my mind on you, not Catherine. You knew you'd have me aroused all night.'

'Were you?' She looked pleased. 'Really? Aroused all night?'

'Minx.' He devoured her mouth, aroused immediately from just the thought of how she'd looked in them. 'Of course I was.'

'I sat up all night, waiting for you,' she said huskily, lifting herself against him when he drew back. 'I knew I was being selfish but I was going to tell you I loved you. I was going to promise to be very tidy and I was going to tell you I'd get used to your horrible duvets. And I do want your babies, Josh. Soon. I'm going to try and be wonderful for you—'

'You're wonderful for me already,' he said, cutting her off. 'I love you for the way you are, Paige. I've always loved you for that. I don't want you to change.'

'What did you want to talk to David about?'

'What do you think?' He tilted her chin up and kissed her mouth again, tasted her. 'I wanted to ask him about this woman who's been driving me crazy. I wanted to see if he had any tips.'

'And?'

'He said you'll drive me crazy,' he said lightly. 'He said you're hell to live with. He said that, as far as he knew, you'd never been on time in your life. He said not to let you cook because you'll smear food from one end of the house to the other, and he said that if I ever put food away to eat later then I should just forget about it because it will always be gone when I come back for it. And he said you'll fill the house with enough expensive flowers to bankrupt me within six months.'

'I'll kill him,' Paige snarled.

'I didn't listen to him,' he finished softly. 'But I did ask him to be best man. I'm not waiting for you any longer, Paige. It's your wedding I was talking about in three or four weeks. I'm not going to be Mr Patience any more.'

'You have never, Josh, been Mr Patience,' she whispered. 'That is a shameful distortion of the truth. Mr Impatience, perhaps. Mr Irritated. Mr Exasperated. Mr If-you-dare-go-near-that-washing-machine-I-will-beat-you-silly, perhaps.'

'But you love me anyway.'

'I love you anyway.' She kissed him, softly. 'Mmm. You feel good. Sex, please. Now.'

'You'll have to wait until the cycle finishes,' he said firmly, glancing towards the washing machine. 'You're not leaving this room while that's still going.'

'Well, if you insist.' With a careless smile she hauled her T-shirt over her head and threw it towards the sink, quickly followed by her skirt. 'Against the wall, darling Josh. Or would you prefer the floor? Or how about on top of the machine?'

'Shameless floozy.' He laughed but his breath caught in his throat as she launched herself at him. 'Let's try all three.'

MILLS & BOON®

Makes any time special™

Mills & Boon publish 29 new titles every month. Select from...

Modern Romance™   Tender Romance™

Sensual Romance™

Medical Romance™ Historical Romance™

MAT2

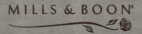

Medical Romance™

BAUBLES, BELLS AND BOOTEES *by Meredith Webber*

Love had grown for Fran when she agreed to marry family friend Dr Henry Griffiths. Knowing how much he wants children, she is distraught at her inability to conceive and decides to find him a new Mrs Griffiths for Christmas.

A KIND OF MAGIC *by Laura MacDonald*

Staff nurse Sophie Quentin's immediate attraction to Benedict, the new registrar, caused her some concern. Even if nothing developed between them, how could she continue her engagement to Miles?

WRAPPED IN TINSEL *by Margaret O'Neill*

Callum Mackintosh's sudden re-appearance after ten years was hardly the Christmas surprise Nan Winters had wanted. But she wasn't in a position to turn down a locum doctor…

On sale 1 December 2000

FREE!

4 Books
and a surprise gift!

We would like to take this opportunity to thank you for reading this Mills & Boon® book by offering you the chance to take FOUR more specially selected titles from the Medical Romance™ series absolutely FREE! We're also making this offer to introduce you to the benefits of the Reader Service™ —

★ FREE home delivery
★ FREE gifts and competitions
★ FREE monthly Newsletter
★ Books available before they're in the shops
★ Exclusive Reader Service discounts

Accepting these FREE books and gift places you under no obligation to buy; you may cancel at any time, even after receiving your free shipment. Simply complete your details below and return the entire page to the address below. *You don't even need a stamp!*

YES! Please send me 4 free Medical Romance books and a surprise gift. I understand that unless you hear from me, I will receive 6 superb new titles every month for just £2.40 each, postage and packing free. I am under no obligation to purchase any books and may cancel my subscription at any time. The free books and gift will be mine to keep in any case.

M0ZEB

Ms/Mrs/Miss/Mr ....Initials ....
BLOCK CAPITALS PLEASE

Surname...

Address..

....

....Postcode ....

Send this whole page to:
UK: The Reader Service, FREEPOST CN81, Croydon, CR9 3WZ
EIRE: The Reader Service, PO Box 4546, Kilcock, County Kildare (stamp required)